LOVE LIKE THEM

love like Them

CANDACE PARKER

DEDICATION

For my husband. My days of writing about the possibilities of love have ended now that you have shown me they can be a reality.

Chapter 1

"THEY SAY WHEN YOU KNOW, YOU KNOW," SAWYER Reynolds tells the sea of faces—217, to be exact—staring back at her. "That you meet someone and think, *there* you are. That you look into this person's eyes and feel like you just walked through your front door after a cold and rainy day."

She turns to her best friend and her brand-new husband, who are sitting at a table full of pink and blue hydrangeas and dabbing at their eyes with tissues.

"That's exactly how Ava felt when she met Mike," Sawyer continues. "She just *knew*. And clearly, so did our handsome groom!"

Some of the guests begin to clap softly. Ava lets out an audible sniffle. Couples all around the room pull their significant others closer.

Sawyer feels a knot in her stomach and a lump begins to form in her throat. This is the perfect time to end the speech, she knows. To congratulate the happy newlyweds and disappear back into her seat at table three. But the sight of Ava's little sister—who is also like her own little sister—kissing her disgustingly hot doctor husband while holding her pregnant belly fills Sawyer with a wave of despair. She raises the microphone again.

"Of course, sometimes you're wrong," she says. "Sometimes you *think* you know. You *think* you've met your person. And then he takes up goat yoga. *Goat* yoga! And you know what he does? He falls for the hippie-dippy instructor and dumps you, just like that!"

The room falls eerily silent, all 217 faces staring at her with wide eyes. Just as Sawyer's knees begin to buckle, she feels an arm around her, gently pulling her up. It's Ava, resplendent in her strapless white gown.

"Come on, Seesaw," Ava whispers, using the nickname she'd given Sawyer on the school playground back in kindergarten. "Let's get you some water."

But Sawyer looks at her friend, who's being so supportive even though Sawyer just screwed up her maid-of-honor speech, and knows that she can't end it this way. She takes a deep breath and slings her arm around Ava's shoulders, then looks back out at the crowd.

"But sometimes you're right," she continues. "Sometimes you lock eyes with someone in the kindergarten block corner and think, *there* you are. And that person becomes your very best friend. Your ride or die. The one who celebrates with you when you fall in love, lifts you up when you get your heart broken and drives you to 7-11 in the middle of the night because you just *need* a pack of those tiny little powdered donuts.

When I met Ava, I just knew. And when I met Mike, I just knew—that he is the perfect man for her. That they'll take care of each other and make each other happy for the rest of their lives. I have never been so sure of anything. So, to Ava and Mike—may your marriage be filled with love, success and joy!"

As Champagne glasses clink and the wedding guests cheer, Sawyer and Ava clutch each other tightly and ugly cry.

"I love you so much, Seesaw," splutters Ava.

"I love you, too!"

Suddenly, Ava's Aunt Grace appears. "All right, girls—we don't need anyone's mascara to run all over anyone's dress," she says. "Get back to that fine specimen of yours, Ava. Sawyer, let's take a walk to the bar."

Chapter 2

"TWO GIN AND TONICS, PLEASE," AUNT GRACE TELLS the bartender, a paunchy man who appears to be in his sixties. She gives him a little wink, and Sawyer sees his cheeks turn pink.

"I'm not sure I should drink much tonight," Sawyer says.

"Nonsense!" Aunt Grace replies. "You're as young as this night is!"

"I'm 29," Sawyer replies.

"A spring chicken!"

The bartender slides the two glasses across the bar, and Aunt Grace passes one to Sawyer. They clink glasses and each take a sip. Sawyer winces and gives a little shudder. Aunt Grace smiles and lets out an, "Aaaahh," as if she just took a refreshing sip of lemonade.

Aunt Grace looks as striking as ever in a form-fitting burgundy lace dress, her dark wavy curls bouncing around her shoulders and her make-up flawless. The first time Sawyer met her was in first grade, when Aunt Grace moved in with Ava's family for a few months after her divorce. Sawyer thought she was the most beautiful woman she had ever seen and asked Ava if she was a supermodel. When Ava told her Aunt Grace was a professional makeup artist, she seemed even cooler in Sawyer's eyes.

Over the years, Aunt Grace had married twice more. Neither of the marriages had lasted very long, and that's when Aunt Grace realized marriage wasn't for her. She worked hard to make ends meet for several years until she made a name for herself in the makeup industry and began to travel the world doing makeup for fashion shows. Now, at 57, Aunt Grace was semi-retired and living her best life. Ava had always worried she'd end up lonely, but Aunt Grace was never without a man by her side.

"Now listen to me, honey," Aunt Grace tells Sawyer, leaning in so close she could smell her Dior perfume. "You're obviously still upset over that Gavin guy. It's time for you to put on your big-girl panties and move on."

"But the breakup was only three weeks ago," Sawyer says. "I thought he was *the one*."

"See, that's your problem right there. You put too much expectation into what you call 'relationships.' You want my advice? Date like a man."

"Date like a *man*?" Sawyer asks, taking another sip of her drink. "What's that supposed to mean?"

"It means having no expectations," Aunt Grace replies. "Stop planning your wedding the minute you meet a man. Stop being so *needy*. Just have fun. Live in the moment. Enjoy the good parts of dating without all the drama. You'll save yourself a lot of unnecessary heartache."

As if on cue, a tall, attractive man in a well-fitted navy suit appears. He smiles brightly at Sawyer and Aunt Grace.

"*There* you are!" he says.

Sawyer's heart skips a beat. Navy Suit looks to be about her age—if not a few years younger—and was obviously listening to her speech. Sawyer is about to introduce herself when Aunt Grace plops her drink down onto the bar and throws her arms around Navy Suit's neck.

"*Here* I am!" she replies. "I was just giving some advice to my pseudo niece, here."

The man gives Sawyer a small wave and then looks at Aunt Grace. "The band started up again," he tells her. "I need my dance partner back."

As he grabs Aunt Grace's hand and begins to pull her back into the ballroom, she glances back at Sawyer and raises her eyebrows. "See what I mean? Date like *him*!"

Sawyer guzzles the rest of her gin and tonic and slams it down on the bar, coming face to face with the bartender.

"Screw my life," she tells him. She picks up Aunt Grace's glass and knocks the rest of that drink back too.

Chapter 3

TWO HOURS LATER SAWYER SITS ALONE AT TABLE three in her baby pink cocktail dress that now has red wine splattered down the front. The rest of her tablemates—Ava's two college friends and two cousins, who served as bridesmaids—are dancing with their husbands and boyfriends to "Stay With You" by John Legend. The empty spot to Sawyer's left, which was supposed to be Gavin's seat, is still pristine. Sawyer gently tips her red wine onto the spot in protest, watching the liquid bleed into the crisp white tablecloth.

She glances at the dance floor. Her best friend is gazing up into Mike's eyes with unbridled joy. Navy Suit is twirling Aunt Grace around flamboyantly, not at all to the beat of the song, as she throws her head back with laughter. It seems, in fact, that nearly every single guest—except for the kids, Ava's 95-year-old grandparents and a few random people at table 21—are on the dance floor.

That's it, Sawyer decides. She gulps down the rest of her wine, unhooks her purse from the back of her chair and stands up. She feels a little wobbly from all the alcohol, but she is determined to get some fresh air. She'd done her maid of honor duties: She threw her arms in the air and danced to Beyoncé with Ava, she schmoozed with Ava and Mike's entire families—even the weird uncles—and she oohed and aahed over the couple's baby pictures during the slideshow Ava's mom put together. She figured she could ride out the last hour or so of the reception outside, then slip back in at the end to say her goodbyes. No one would ever notice.

On her way past the bar, the paunchy bartender lifts a hand in greeting. "Another gin and tonic?"

She glances down at her wine-stained dress.

"Um, sure—a gin and tonic, please," she replies. He hands her the drink and says, "Don't worry, sweetheart. Your prince will come."

Sawyer grabs it and hurries outside. Things are bad when even the paunchy bartender feels sorry for you.

She steps out into the warm summer evening and soaks in the scenery. She spots a stone path to her right, with a white gazebo at the end. She hobbles over to the gazebo in her silver kitten heels and is thrilled to find wooden benches inside. She plops down, kicks off her heels and sighs.

Aunt Grace was right—Sawyer *did* put too much expectation on the men she dated. And, as much as she hated to admit it, she *was* too needy.

Sawyer had dated Derrick, a football player, all through high school. They had applied to all the same colleges so they could stay together and had both chosen the University of North Carolina. Sawyer figured they'd date all through college, move back to Ridgewood (the New Jersey suburb they'd grown up in), get married and have kids. But halfway through freshman year, Derrick broke up with her, saying he wanted to have "the full college experience." Looking back, Sawyer realizes that UNC was actually Derrick's first choice, not hers, and that he probably would have gone there even if she'd chosen not to.

Sawyer had two more long-term relationships in her twenties. She dated Brad, a law student, for nearly two years until one day, after watching her coo over one too many babies at the mall, he told her over their Panda Express lunch at the food court that he never wanted to have kids. She obsessed over it for two weeks before breaking up with him, saying she couldn't give up the prospect of having children. The last she'd heard (or seen on Facebook, rather) was that Brad had married a fellow lawyer in Connecticut and had three sons.

Later, Sawyer had an 18-month relationship with a financial planner named Drew. He was handsome, kind and made a lot of money. But they started fighting a lot after it became clear he had no plans to move in with Sawyer. The biggest argument came after he discovered some tees and underwear Sawyer had left in one of his dresser drawers. She stuffed them in a bag, stormed out and they never spoke again.

After that, Sawyer threw herself into her job as a marketing associate and vowed never to let herself get close to another man. She was single for two years when she met Gavin at a bar. Like her exes, he was handsome and successful, with a high-powered job at an investment firm. On top of that, he was older than Sawyer and had seemed just as determined to settle down.

Six months later, the higher-ups at Gavin's firm realized how overworked and exhausted their employees were. So, the firm introduced a new wellness program, partnering with local businesses to allow its employees to attend free health classes—including goat yoga. When Gavin arrived at Sawyer's apartment one evening smelling like goats, she laughed at him before shoving him into the bathroom to shower. When the same thing happened a month later, he didn't even make it to the shower before telling her the goat yoga instructor was his "twin flame" and that he was moving in with her so they could live a life of "love and light." As Sawyer began to toss his things at him angrily, he simply bowed to her with his hands in prayer and said "namaste" before turning and leaving.

Later that night, through heaving sobs at Ava's house, Sawyer had vowed never to date again. But now, Aunt Grace had made her realize that she didn't have to stop dating. She just needed to change *how* and *whom* she dated. From now on, she wouldn't look for guys with good jobs because they seemed like marriage material. Instead, she'd look for guys who were *fun*. Guys she could laugh with. And she'd take things one day at a time, without a second thought as to where things were going.

Chapter 4

SAWYER IS DEBATING WHETHER TO HEAD INSIDE FOR another drink when she hears footsteps. She looks up to see a man in a tuxedo standing in the gazebo's entrance. He is boyishly handsome, with deep blue eyes, a youthful grin and dirty-blond wavy hair. His bowtie hangs loosely around his neck and his top two buttons are undone, revealing a bit of tattoo on the side of his neck. Sawyer feels her heart begin to pound.

"Are you a surfer dude?" she asks as he enters the gazebo and sits across from her. She immediately winces, realizing she's more drunk than she'd thought. But the man's smile grows wider, and he doesn't miss a beat.

"That depends—do you want me to be?"

He holds her gaze, his blue eyes boring into her brown ones. Did it just get hotter outside?

"I want you to be whoever *you* want to be," she replies. She's doing it. She's flirting.

"I only want to be myself," he replies. He gets up and walks across the gazebo to sit next to Sawyer. He reaches his hand out. "I'm Ethan."

She takes his hand and feels a bolt of electricity shoot up her arm. "Sawyer," she replies.

His eyes stay locked on hers as he offers a dazzling smile. "It's very nice to meet you, Sawyer."

She giggles.

"What's so funny? Do I have something in my teeth? A massive booger hanging out of my nose?" he asks, which makes her snort.

"No, no, you're fine," she tells him. "You're good. You look good. I guess I've just had too much to drink. How about you?"

"Me? No, I haven't had a single drink."

"*What*?! I can't get through a wedding without having a drink."

"Well, I can't get through a wedding if I *do* have a drink."

Sawyer is about to question him, but finds herself consumed with thoughts of what table Ethan is at and how she has managed not to see him until now. Worse, she wonders if he is here with a date. Instinctively she glances down at his left hand. No ring. He follows her gaze and glances at her left hand, then up into her eyes.

"So ... what do you think?" he asks her.

"A-about what?" She tries to hide the fact that she is trembling.

He nods his head toward the parking lot.

"Should we get out of here?" he asks. "Go get a drink?"

Sawyer isn't sure what to say. This is her best friend's wedding. She can't just *leave*. Never mind the fact that this man—this gorgeous, funny, sexy man—is a complete stranger to her. Haven't her parents taught her never to get in a car with a strange man?

And yet, it's impossible for her to deny the powerful force pulling her toward Ethan. She feels it in her bones; this overwhelming need to be right next to him. She may have just met him, but when she looks into those blue eyes she certainly does not see a stranger. And then there's the frightening thought that if she goes back inside—if she lets this moment get away—she'll never get this chance back.

She glances back toward the door to the banquet hall, then down at her watch.

"C'mon," he says. "There's less than an hour left anyway. Let's go have some fun."

She feels her pulse quickening even more. It's such a rush, this feeling. Like the world is alive with possibility. Like if she goes with Ethan, her life will change forever.

"I don't know…" she tells him.

"Well, I do," he says. "I just know."

And that does it. Those three words. An image of Ava—radiant, joyful Ava—flashes through Sawyer's mind. Ava is in there with the love of her life. Sawyer knows in her heart that Ava would not want her to let this moment pass.

Before she can change her mind, Sawyer stands up and slings her purse over her shoulder.

"OK," she says. "Let's go."

Ethan reaches down and grabs her kitten heels. "Allow me."

As Sawyer stands there in her wine-stained pink gown, watching this handsome man slide her shoes onto her feet Cinderella-style, she can't help but laugh at the fairy tale of it all.

Chapter 5

FIFTEEN MINUTES LATER, SHE'S SITTING BESIDE Ethan in his gray Honda Civic as they head back to the city. She already texted Ava to let her know that she loves her, that she won't need a ride home from Mike's brother and that she'll explain later. Then she turned her phone off and slid it back into her purse.

Sawyer can't stop stealing glances at Ethan's chiseled profile out of the corner of her eye. She is struck by how magical, yet comfortable, all of this feels. She reached over and changed the XM radio station from classic rock to pop as soon as he started the car, like she'd been sitting in the passenger seat for years. He cringed, but kept the pop station on. And yet, she can't seem to work up the nerve to grab his right hand, which is resting on the center console.

"So, how long have you known Mike?" she asks him.

"Why are you assuming it's Mike that I know?"

"Because if it was Ava, then I'd have met you already."

He doesn't respond, which drives Sawyer just a little crazy. "But seriously—how long have you known him?" she asks.

"Well," he responds, keeping his eyes on the road. "I just met him tonight."

"*What?* What do you mean? Did you blow off your *date?*"

He chuckles, then reaches over and places his hand gently on her knee. She tries to ignore the warmth she feels between her legs. "No, I did not," he replies. "Actually, I wasn't a wedding guest."

Images of Vince Vaughn and Owen Wilson flash through Sawyer's mind. "Are you a *wedding crasher?*"

Ethan laughs so hard the car swerves a bit. "Sorry!" he says. "That's hilarious. No, I'm not a wedding crasher. I was working. Bartending. I was on one of my breaks when I came out to the gazebo."

"You weren't bartending," Sawyer says. "The old guy was bartending."

"Ah, good old Frank," Ethan says. "He's at the bar near the entrance. Lucky bastard gets the most tips. I'm at the bar on the left of the room. There's also a bar in the back."

So *that* explains how Sawyer hadn't seen him. But if Ethan was working…

"You were on a break," she tells him. "So, what? You just decided to leave without even saying anything? Without getting paid? Why would you *do* that?"

He shrugs, and she can see his shoulder muscles ripple through his shirt (he'd taken his tuxedo jacket off as soon as they got in the car). "I wasn't planning on it," he replies. "But I wasn't planning on meeting you, either."

Sawyer leans her head back against the seat and exhales sharply. Spontaneity of that magnitude has always made her uncomfortable. She's just not used to it. All her life, Sawyer has been a planner. She majored in Communication at UNC, then landed a job as a marketing assistant at a small firm after she graduated. She worked her way up to marketing associate at that firm before moving to Savoy, the largest marketing firm in New York City. She had the same title, but a big jump in pay. She eventually won the firm's grad school scholarship and enrolled at Fordham University to earn her master's degree in Marketing Intelligence. She had just completed her first year and only had one year to go before she could head one of the departments at Savoy.

Sawyer would have never come this far if she hadn't stuck to a specific plan she'd set for herself. And part of that plan was finding a successful man, one who was established in his career and had some direction in life.

But look at where that had gotten her. She's 29 and single after yet another failed relationship. All these successful men had done was disappoint her.

She remembers Aunt Grace's words—date like a man. She looks over at Ethan, drumming the steering wheel along to a Taylor Swift song, totally unphased about walking out on his job. He looks carefree, content and completely comfortable in his own skin. Sawyer isn't sure she wants to be like him, but she sure as hell wants to be *around* him.

She lifts her head and grabs his hand. "So … where are we going?"

Chapter 6

HE TAKES HER TO A SPEAKEASY FULL OF ARTIST TYPES that's hidden down a long flight of wooden stairs beneath a used bookstore. Of *course* Ethan knows about a place like this, she thinks to herself. The vibe is laid-back and funky, with dim lighting, posters of classic book covers lining the walls, stacks of board games with torn boxes in the corners and beanbag chairs scattered around low wooden tables.

Sawyer and Ethan are grossly overdressed, but no one even gives them a second glance as they select one of the tables and sit. After a server brings them two Miller High Lifes, they settle into conversation. Sawyer learns that Ethan is 31, loves to read and go to cafes, and works out every day (obviously).

"How long have you been bartending?" Sawyer asks.

"Longer than I'd like," Ethan admits. "About two years now."

"And … are you worried about finding another job now? Worried that you maybe … burned some bridges?"

Ethan shrugs. "Ya know, bartending obviously isn't my passion. I just kinda fell into it when I left my job in corporate America."

"And what was your job?"

"One that offered me no fulfillment whatsoever—marketing."

Sawyer nearly spits out her drink as she bursts into laughter.

"What's so funny?" he asks.

"Well …" she replies. "Marketing is *my* job. My passion. I'm actually going for my master's in marketing so I can head up a department at my firm."

At that, Ethan starts laughing too.

"Now *that* is funny," he says. "I actually have my master's in marketing. Climbed the ladder quickly at my firm. Became a VP really young. I made a lot of money, but the job brought me no joy. I worked pretty long hours and just wasn't passionate about what I did. One day I decided life was just too short to work so hard at a job I didn't love. So I walked into my boss's office and quit right on the spot. I told him I'd give him a month to find my replacement. He was in shock, and he tried for weeks to talk me out of it. But once I'd made up my mind, there was no turning back."

Sawyer is transfixed by Ethan's every word. She feels so many things—awe at his courage. Envy at his confidence. Concerned that he'd wasted his master's degree and walked away from such an amazing job. But most of all, she's curious. She wants to know everything about Ethan, to drink all of him in.

"So … what *is* your passion?" she asks him.

For just a moment, she sees a flash of vulnerability in his eyes.

"I'd tell you, but you'll laugh at me."

She reaches across the table and places her hand on his, feeling warmth crash over her body like an ocean wave. "I promise I won't laugh at you."

He turns his hand over and laces his fingers through hers. "OK, well … I want to start my own business. I saved a lot of money during my marketing days and wasn't quite sure what I'd do with it. But I got this business idea right before I quit. I knew it would take a lot of time and effort to make it happen, so I started doing all sorts of odd jobs— bartending, waiting tables, Uber driving—to save more money while I took courses to get some of the certifications I need. I finally feel like I might be getting somewhere now, but there's a lot of competition out there. So, we'll see."

"I'm confused," Sawyer replies. "Why would I laugh at you for wanting to start your own business?"

"Well," he says. "The business is ... a yoga studio."

He looks up into her eyes, where she is sure he can register her shock. She doesn't know what to think or what to say. The irony of it all—a *yoga* studio, of all things.

"I know, I know," he says quickly. "Yoga is not very 'manly.' I've gotten a lot of grief from my friends for it. But it has helped me through so many things ... made me stronger ... given me balance ..."

He trails off when he notices Sawyer shaking. He wonders if she is having a seizure when suddenly, she explodes into violent laughter. She clutches her stomach and gasps for air as tears roll down her cheeks. He glares at her as she begins to fan herself with her hand.

"I fucking knew it," he says angrily. "I knew you were gonna laugh at me!" He slides his chair back and stands up, but Sawyer grabs at his arm.

"No, wait. Ethan, wait. I'm sorry," she says. "I wasn't laughing at you, I promise. Please. Sit down."

He hesitates a moment before sinking back down into his seat. "It sure looks like you were laughing at me."

"I wasn't. But if I tell you why I was laughing, do you promise not to laugh at *me*?"

He raises an eyebrow at her. "After that little display, I can't make any promises."

"Fair enough." She takes a deep breath. "So, I just got out of a relationship three weeks ago. I had my heart broken pretty badly."

He takes a sip of his second Miller High Life, which the bartender had slipped onto the table during Sawyer's laughing fit. "OK," he says. "Why would I laugh at that?"

"Well … he dumped me because he fell for another woman."

"Ouch," Ethan says. "Who was she? His secretary? Neighbor? Travel agent?"

"None of the above," Sawyer says. "She was his goat yoga instructor."

Ethan stares at her quietly, then contorts his face into an expression that looks like he just drank curdled milk. Sawyer wonders if he's having a heart attack. And then she realizes he's just trying hard—really, really hard—not to laugh.

"OK, fine—just do it," she says. "Let it all out."

He bursts into laughter and before long, Sawyer is laughing too.

"*Goat* yoga?" he splutters. "What the hell is *goat* yoga?"

"I don't know!" Sawyer replies through giggles. "But I bet you anyone in this room can tell you! I just know that he smelled like shit every time he came home from it."

This sets Ethan over the edge, and when the waiter comes over and asks pointedly if he can get them anything else, he and Sawyer realize they're not supporting the chill vibe of the speakeasy. He looks at her. "Wanna come to my place for a nightcap?"

She feels her heart flutter. "Heck yeah, I do!"

Chapter 7

THE NEXT MORNING, SAWYER IS STARTLED OUT OF A deep sleep by a hardcover book hitting the floor. She leans over the side of the bed and squints at its title: *Advanced Yoga Volume 3*. She doesn't remember buying that book. Was it one Ava had brought over last month? What a cruel gift to give someone who'd recently been dumped for a goat yogi!

But then the culprit of the falling book saunters by—a tabby cat named Calvin—and Sawyer quickly realizes she's not at her third-floor apartment in Hoboken. She's at Ethan's ground-floor studio in Williamsburg, Brooklyn—and a quick peek under the covers confirms that she is, in fact, naked.

Oh my God, oh my God, oh my God, Sawyer thinks. Her heart begins to race as memories from last night flash into her mind: Ethan's breath in her ear as he whispered, "I want to know every part of you." His soft lips grazing the spots on her body that men before had barely noticed, like the freckle inside her right thigh. And those blue eyes staring deeply into hers as he entered her, moving gently at first but then with more and more intensity.

Sawyer shudders with a mix of pleasure and panic. She rolls over. Sure enough, there's Ethan. He's lying on his back fast asleep, half turned toward her with his right arm under his pillow. She stares at him for several minutes, admiring the curve of his jawbone and the fullness of his lips. She's jarred by both the intensity of her attraction to him and how normal it feels to be waking up beside him. Like she's known him forever. Like she's woken up in this bed on thousands of other sunny mornings just like this one.

But then, some less pleasant memories take over: Crying hysterically in the shower the evening Gavin left. Sleepless nights curled up in bed after each breakup, wondering why another man couldn't seem to love her enough. All those days she'd spent consumed by heartache, loneliness and fear.

She reaches out her hand and gently touches Ethan's cheek. She has never before felt so comfortable so quickly with any man. She has never before *connected* so strongly with any man.

But at the same time, she trusted all those other men. She believed in them. And they all let her down. So how can she be sure she isn't wrong about Ethan? How can she be sure he won't let her down, too?

Then she remembers Aunt Grace's advice: "Date like a man." And that's when her resolve takes over.

I can't do this again, Sawyer thinks as her heart begins to pound wildly. *I can't set myself up to be hurt again. This strong connection I feel is not real. It's just the rush from a night of good fun and mind-blowing sex. That's all it is.*

Before she can change her mind, Sawyer jumps out of the bed and hastily gathers the oversize T-shirt and drawstring sweats Ethan gave her when they got back to his apartment. She ducks into the bathroom and gets dressed as quickly and quietly as possible, silently praying he won't wake up. She knows if he does, it will be nearly impossible to leave. She tiptoes back out of the bathroom and glances at the bed, where Ethan hasn't moved.

Sawyer grabs her purse and shoes and takes a step toward the apartment door. Then she turns and tiptoes back to the desk, where she finds a pen and notepad.

E — thank you for a magical night. I will never forget you. -S

She takes one last look at Ethan as a single tear drips down her left cheek. Then she steps gingerly over a resting Calvin and slips out the door, leaving only her maid of honor dress behind.

Chapter 8

"SO—YOU JUST *LEFT*?" AVA ASKS, TAKING A SIP OF her margarita. "You didn't even leave your phone number?"

Sawyer shrugs. "I didn't want to go through it again, Ava. Waiting by my phone: 'Will he call? Won't he call?' So I took Aunt Grace's advice and just had fun. That's all it was. Just a fun night with some amazing sex."

Ava sighs and shakes her head. "Aunt Grace is thrice divorced and single at nearly 60, Seesaw. She's hardly a dating expert. And besides— even men who casually date don't just walk away from mind-blowing sex. Have I taught you *nothing*?"

Sawyer giggles. A little over three weeks has passed since her night with Ethan, and it's her first time seeing Ava, who returned from her lengthy Hawaiian honeymoon two days earlier. With Ava away and Ethan constantly invading her thoughts like a relentless gnat, it had been a tough couple weeks for Sawyer. She felt strangely unsettled and had a hard time sleeping, but she fought her exhaustion to meet Ava after work for their biweekly Margarita Monday. Now that she's sitting across from her bestie at their favorite Mexican spot in SoHo, she feels centered again.

"OK, enough about Ethan," Sawyer says. "I want to hear *every-thing*. How was the honeymoon? How was Hawaii? Was it *amazing*?"

"It was great, Seesaw," Ava says, dipping a chip into a bowl of salsa.

"*Great*? That's it? Just great?"

"It was magical, OK?" Ava admits. "I'm just tired, that's all. I don't know *why* I thought it would be a good idea to go back to work while I'm still jet lagged. You know how many emails I had to go through today? 1,371!"

"Boo hoo hoo. I feel *so* sorry for you," Sawyer replies, and the two burst into giggles as the server appears with their fajitas.

"Another round, ladies?"

There's no hesitation before they respond in unison. "Absolutely!"

Chapter 9

ONE HOUR AND ONE MARGARITA LATER, AVA HOLDS Sawyer's long dark hair back as Sawyer vomits into a toilet in the restaurant's bathroom.

"Oh my *God*," Sawyer moans, gasping for air. "What the hell is *happening* to me? I only had two drinks! And you ate the same food as me!"

"I don't know, Seesaw," Ava replies. "Maybe you caught a bug or something. But I'm calling Mike and telling him I'm sleeping at your place tonight. I can't let you go home by yourself like this."

They take an Uber back to Hoboken. Though Sawyer doesn't get sick again, she is weeping uncontrollably by the time the car pulls up to her apartment building. "I'm such an idiot, Ava! Why wouldn't I leave him my number? He was perfect! And now I'll never know what might have been!"

"You are *so* going to ruin my five-star rating," Ava grumbles as the driver roars away, mumbling under his breath about needing a new job.

They head upstairs into Ava's bedroom to change. Sawyer opens her pajama drawer and tries to avoid looking at Ethan's clothing, which she had washed and shoved into the back of the drawer. She hasn't been able to bring herself to get rid of them. She glances over at Ava, who is digging through the bottom dresser drawer.

"You're a married woman now," she tells Ava. "Don't you think you should take your stuff home and give me my drawer back?"

"Oh, shut it," Ava replies, tossing a dirty sock at Sawyer. Then she pauses. "Oh, shit. I forgot to put tampons in my purse. Do you have one?"

"You know where they are," Sawyer replies. She plops into bed as Ava heads into the bathroom, feeling too tired to even wash her face or brush her teeth. She's just starting to drift off to sleep when Ava reappears, her eyes wild.

"What's the matter?" Sawyer asks sleepily.

"You're out of tampons!" Ava replies.

"Oh, man," Sawyer replies. "Good thing the 24-hour Duane Reade is on my corner."

"I *know* that, Seesaw!" Ava replies. "But how? *How* are you out of tampons?"

"Gimme a break, girl. I've been a bit preoccupied," Sawyer replies, yawning.

"Too preoccupied to notice that you missed your period?" Ava asks. "C'mon, Seesaw—you know we always get our periods at the same time!"

"I—," Sawyer begins. She suddenly realizes what Ava is trying to tell her and bolts upright in the bed. "Oh, *shit*! Shit shit *shit*!" She begins to fan her hands maniacally in front of her face.

"OK, OK—calm down," Ava says, sitting on the bed next to Sawyer. "Let's not jump to conclusions. You did use a condom with Ethan, right?"

"Of *course* we did!" Sawyer snaps. "But maybe it broke." She stands up and begins to pace back and forth.

"You would know if the condom broke."

"Well I *don't* know, OK?! I had a lot to drink! I don't even remember falling asleep. I just remember waking up in his bed the next morning and panicking."

Ava stands up and grabs Sawyer's keys off the nightstand.

"Where are you going?" Sawyer asks.

"Where do you think I'm going? I'm going to buy a pregnancy test. And tampons."

As the front door clicks behind Ava, Sawyer slumps back onto the bed and pulls her pillow over her head.

Please no, she thinks. *Please don't let me pregnant. I'm starting grad school again next week. I live in a one-bedroom apartment. This can't be happening. I can't be pregnant!*

Chapter 10

"YOU'RE *PREGNANT*!" AVA SQUEALS, BURSTING OUT of the bathroom and holding the pee stick in front of her like Mufasa presenting baby Simba.

Sawyer stands up from the couch, where she'd been sitting and furiously shaking her leg while Ava awaited the results of the pregnancy test. She can feel the blood rush from her face.

"I'm … *what*?"

Ava throws her arms around Sawyer. "You're pregnant, Seesaw. I can't believe it. I'm going to be an aunt!"

"No. *No no no no no no no*," Sawyer says, pacing maniacally. "This can't be real, Ava. I'm not pregnant."

Ava holds out the test again. "Two lines, Seesaw. You're pregnant."

Sawyer bursts into tears and throws herself back onto the couch. "No. *No no no no no no no*!"

Ava sits beside her. "Seesaw, calm down. I know this is a lot …"

"A lot?" Sawyer shouts. "A *lot*?! I'm *pregnant*, Ava! From a one-night stand! And I have no way of getting in touch with the father because I freakin' walked out on him! I don't know his number. I don't know his last name …"

"I will find him for you," Ava says. "I will call the catering hall. I will go to his apartment in Brooklyn if I have to …"

"But what if you can't find him?" Sawyer sobs. "Or worse, what if you do find him, and he wants nothing to do with me? Then what? My baby will grow up without a father!"

"She'll still have all the love she needs. She'll have your family. She'll have me and Mike. And she'll have *you*."

"*She?*"

Ava smiles. "Yes, *she*. She'll be a little girl, and maybe Mike and I will get pregnant right away, and have a daughter and they'll grow up to be besties. Just like us."

"I have dreams, Ava! I want to get my master's degree and move up at my company. I want to get married. And *then* I want to have kids. I can't be a single mom!"

"Seesaw, when have you ever *not* been able to do something?" Ava asks. "You'll have so much help, and we'll figure it out. I promise."

Ava puts her arm around Sawyer and pulls her close. The two girls sit and weep until Sawyer falls asleep on Ava's shoulder.

Chapter 11

"*AAAAAAAAHHHHHHHHHHH*!" SAWYER WAILS AS SHE pushes with all her might. Her mother and Ava are on opposite sides of the hospital bed, holding Sawyer's hands and fighting the urge to cry out in pain themselves.

"You're doing so great," the young female doctor tells her. "Let's take a few breaths, and then we'll start pushing again."

Thirty-nine weeks and five days have passed in a flurry of baby preparations and heightened emotions. The day after Sawyer found out she was pregnant, Ava had called the catering hall to ask about Ethan. The manager refused to reveal his last name due to their privacy policy, but once she heard the situation, she shared Ethan's cellphone number. When Sawyer finally worked up the nerve to call a week later, she found that the number had been disconnected.

So, Sawyer and Ava took an Uber to Brooklyn that weekend. Ava rang the doorbell while Sawyer crouched behind a bush, watching the scene unfold. Her heart sank when a leggy blonde woman answered the door. But when Ava asked for Ethan, the blonde said she didn't know any Ethans and that she had just moved in a week prior.

It took Ava a month of Internet research, social media sleuthing and hanging flyers in Williamsburg before she, like Sawyer, gave up on the idea of ever finding Ethan. By that point, Sawyer had convinced herself that his disappearance was a sign she wasn't meant to find him after all. Her parents' excitement about becoming grandparents (despite the less-than-ideal circumstances) had also eased her dread about having a baby, and Sawyer made preparing for motherhood her new-found purpose in life.

The first thing she did was talk to Alan, her supervisor, who'd become like a second father to her. He was surprisingly supportive of her plan to defer grad school for a couple years while she got her life in order, and even offered her a small raise and the flexibility to work from home two days a week.

"You've done great work here, Sawyer, and you deserve some happiness," he said. "You'll have your chance to head a department in the future. Just take care of yourself."

Sawyer's parents urged her to move back to Ridgewood so she could be closer to them and to Ava and Mike's new home.

"I can watch the baby while you're at work!" her mother said. "It'll give my life some purpose again!"

Though she loved Hoboken, Sawyer could not pass up this generous offer of free babysitting—or the chance to have her child grow up near his or her grandparents and Auntie Ava. And with the raise, she could afford a two-bedroom apartment in Ridgewood. She figured she could handle the longer commute if it would only be three days a week.

Once Sawyer settled into her new place, the remaining months of her pregnancy passed quickly. She spent her evenings and weekends decorating the nursery with her mom and Ava, strolling the aisles of

Buy Buy Baby and reading every parenting book she could get her hands on.

But now that she was here in the hospital, ready to bring her child into the world, she was once again overcome by fear and uncertainty.

"I can't!" she yelled. "I can't do this!"

"You *can*, sweetheart," her mother assured her.

"Our baby wants to meet us! You got this!" Ava said.

"All right, it's time. Give it one more big push," the doctor said.

Sawyer bears down as hard as she can and lets out a guttural scream that her father and Mike can probably hear from the waiting room down the hall. She feels a stab of pain and then a huge release, followed by a flurry of activity and the urgent cries of a newborn baby. As she catches her breath, she looks into the tearful eyes of Ava, then her mom. A moment later, a nurse places a soft bundle onto her chest.

"Congratulations," the nurse says. "You have a baby boy."

Sawyer peers down into her baby's eyes and is immediately transported back to the first time she met Ethan in the gazebo. Those big, beautiful blue eyes are unmistakably Ethan's. Sawyer feels a wave of love wash over her.

"Hello there, Matthew Ethan Reynolds. I'm your mama." The baby squints back at her. "It's you and me now, kiddo. And I'm going to take such good care of you."

Chapter 12

THREE MONTHS LATER, SAWYER TEETERS OVER TO Ava's black Lexus SUV in her new silver kitten heels. "Oh, *hey* girl!" Ava calls out from the driver's seat. "I see you, looking all fine!"

Sawyer slides into the front seat. "Oh, please. My boobs are saggy, I still haven't lost all the baby weight and I probably have residual spit-up somewhere on my body. You just think I look good because you're not used to seeing me in anything other than yoga pants."

Ava rolls her eyes and begins to drive toward the bus terminal. "So? How do you feel, making your debut back into the world? I feel like I should be playing some Lizzo right now!"

Sawyer fights the urge to cry. "I don't know—I've got mixed feelings. I'm excited to get back to work, but I miss Matthew already. I don't know how I'm gonna be away from him all day."

"You're gonna think about all the fun he's having with grandma and grandpa and how much you're killin' it at work, that's how," Ava replies.

Sawyer sighs. "I just can't believe how quickly 12 weeks of maternity leave flew by."

"Time flies when you're having fun," Ava says.

As soon as they step onto the bus 10 minutes later, Sawyer starts to feel like her old self again. As she looks out the window at the familiar streets, she thinks about how much her life has changed since last year. She never imagined she would be a single mom, living back in the suburbs near her childhood home. But now she can't imagine her life any other way.

Matthew is an absolute dream of a baby. He took to breastfeeding right away and started sleeping through the night at two months old. He is laid-back (like his dad, Sawyer always thinks), happily hanging out on his play mat, in his bouncy seat or basically anywhere else Sawyer chooses to put him. He lets anyone hold him without a fuss and has recently started smiling at everyone, especially his mama. Sawyer is smitten, and though she still feels pangs in her chest whenever she thinks of Ethan (which is quite often), she has come to accept her situation and has convinced herself that things worked out the way they were supposed to.

And Ava and Mike are almost equally in love with Matthew, doting on him and showering him with gifts (which Sawyer likes to remind them are quickly taking over her apartment). They've been actively trying to get pregnant since their honeymoon and haven't had any luck yet, so they recently started seeing a fertility doctor. It's hard for Sawyer not to feel guilty that she accidentally got pregnant during a night of drunken sex with a man she'd just met, while her married best friend is having such a hard time. But Ava never acts bitter about it. Instead, she channels her frustration into her love for Matthew.

"Hel-*lo*! Earth to Sawyer!" Ava says.

"Sorry … what did you say?"

"I *said* I'm excited for Margarita Monday after work!"

Oh, man. Sawyer had forgotten about Margarita Monday. Ava had convinced her that they needed to keep up the tradition—even if it was once a month instead of every other week—and Sawyer's parents had happily agreed to stay with Matthew later on those days. But now Sawyer wishes she hadn't said yes. She's already counting down the minutes until she can see Matthew again.

"Oh, don't even *think* about it," Ava says when Sawyer remains quiet. Ava knows her so well. "You're coming. Especially because Mike is joining us tonight with …"

"With who?" Sawyer asks.

"With no one," Ava replies quickly. "Never mind. C'mon, we're at our stop." She stands up.

"*Ava*! Mike is joining us with *who*?" Sawyer shouts as she chases Ava off the bus.

"I'll see you at 5:15!" Ava calls back, and she disappears into the crowd of commuters.

Chapter 13

SAWYER'S FIRST DAY GOES EXACTLY AS EXPECTED, and she can't believe how good it feels to be back in the office with all her co-workers. Her team takes her to lunch and brings her up to speed on everything she missed, and she manages to get through the day without calling her mother five times to ask about Matthew. She only calls four times—the first when she arrives at the office, the second when she's about to leave for lunch, the third when she returns from lunch and the fourth (a FaceTime call) at 5:15 p.m. while she's standing outside the Mexican restaurant, ready to head inside for Margarita Monday.

"I'm doing gwate, mommy!" Sawyer's mother coos in an exaggerated baby voice as Matthew's squirmy face fills Sawyer's phone screen. "I'm such a good wittle boy, aren't I? I just wuv my gwamma and gwampa, don't I? Yes, I *do*! Yes, I *do*!"

Sawyer ducks her head as a group of passing NYU students snicker.

"Mom, stop! People can *hear* you!"

"Well, it's not my fault I've got the cutest grandson in the world, now is it?" Mrs. Reynolds asks, and her face—or rather, her chin—reappears on the screen. Sawyer sighs. Her parents still haven't quite gotten the hang of FaceTime.

"I'm going inside now. It's going to be a quick dinner. Mike is meeting us and will drive us home. I won't be late."

"Take your time, Sweetie—really," her mother says. "Everything is fine here, and you deserve an evening out. I'm so happy you had a great first day back."

Sawyer smiles. "Thanks, Mom. I'll see you soon."

She enters the restaurant and glances around. "Seesaw! Over here!"

She spots Ava standing next to a table in the far-right corner, waving her arms wildly. As Sawyer approaches, she sees the back of Mike's head. He is sitting across from Ava and next to a dark-haired man. Sawyer's heart stops. She'd forgotten all about her awkward exchange with Ava as they stepped off the bus that morning, and now it hits her—Ava and Mike are trying to set her up.

She glares at Ava as she arrives at the table, and Ava looks back at her with an innocent expression. "I ordered your margarita already!" she chirps in a voice that's a tad too cheery.

"Great," Sawyer replies with decidedly less enthusiasm. She still doesn't sit down.

"Um ... Mike's here!" Ava says brightly, motioning across the table. "And, um, this is his new co-worker, Paul. He decided to join us last minute."

Sawyer gives Ava her best you're-so-full-of-shit look and turns to Mike. "Hey, Mike. Matthew pooped all over the Yankees blanket you bought him." Mike is a die-hard Yankees fan, and Sawyer comes from a long line of Mets fans, so she and Mike have always had a friendly rivalry.

"Wonderful," Mike replies with a chuckle and an eye roll. He turns to his right, where Paul has just stood up to introduce himself. "Paul, this is Sawyer. She is a Mets fan, but I promise she's cool other than that."

"That's OK—I may be able to convert her," Paul says jovially. He sticks out his hand. "I'm Paul Thompson. It's very nice to meet you."

Sawyer finally allows herself to look at Paul and her heart flutters. The man is gorgeous—a cross between Jesse Williams and Alex Rodriguez (still her all-time favorite Yankee). Like Mike and every other guy who works in the financial industry, he is dressed impeccably in a crisp, light blue button-down, charcoal-gray slacks and a pinstriped tie.

"Yes, I …. It's nice to meet you," Sawyer says as she takes his hand.

She looks over at Ava, who is positively beaming. "Well, let's sit down! I'm starving," Ava says.

They sit, exchange some small talk and order their dinners—carne asada tacos for Mike and Paul and chicken fajitas for Sawyer and Ava. When Ava and Mike get into a conversation about Mike's cousin Tony's new girlfriend drama, Paul leans in a little closer to talk to Sawyer. "So, Mike and Ava tell me you have a baby," he says.

"I do! His name is Matthew, and he's three months old. He's the best," Sawyer replies.

Paul smiles. "I've always wanted kids. I still do—badly. I'm 35 now—my clock is ticking!"

Sawyer raises her eyebrows in surprise. It's not every day you meet a man who is so upfront and open about wanting kids. She finds it refreshing. "Why haven't you had them, then?" she asks, and immediately feels Ava nudge her under the table. Sawyer's social skills are awfully rusty, and Ava apparently has one ear on their conversation.

But Paul doesn't skip a beat. "Well, I had two long-term relationships that didn't work out. The first was with my college girlfriend. We started dating freshman year, and we were together almost eight years when she broke up with me. I was wrapped up with business school and getting my career going, and she got tired of waiting for me to propose."

He pauses wistfully for a moment, then continues. "I'm not gonna lie—I was really messed up from that. I spent six months trying to win her back and the next three years working crazy hours and dating here and there. Then I met my last girlfriend. She also worked in the financial industry, and things went really well for two years. But then she got offered her dream job in L.A., and I'd just gotten a big promotion, so I didn't want to leave my company just yet. We gave the long-distance thing the old college try for another year, but it was just too hard to keep things going. I haven't dated anyone seriously since we broke up. It's hard to meet women my age who aren't already married or in a relationship, and most of the younger women I've met aren't looking for anything serious. So, here I am."

Sawyer is quiet for a moment as she takes in everything Paul just said. For so long, it had been the other way around for her. It was her who had wanted something serious and the men who had shied away from commitment.

"I completely understand," she finally tells him. "It's hard to find someone who's on the same page as you. It's going to be even harder for me now that I'm a single mother. Who knows when, or *if*, I'll date again?"

Paul looks directly into her eyes, and she feels a twinge of . . . something. "How about this Saturday?" he asks. "I just scored tickets to *Hamilton* from a buddy who can't go, and I'd love for you to join me. We can grab some dinner first or a drink afterward—whatever works for you."

Sawyer feels her heart begin to race. She can't even remember the last time she'd been out on a Saturday night, much less with a handsome man at the hottest show on Broadway.

"Wow—I … I'd love to," she says. "But I'm not sure my parents will be able to take the baby, and—."

"Mike and I can babysit!" Ava interrupts, no longer pretending not to eavesdrop. "We need some baby time."

"Yeah, Matthew can watch the Yankees game with me," Mike says with a chuckle.

"Well then … is it a date?" Paul asks.

Sawyer looks over at Ava, who nods encouragingly. Then she looks back at Paul and nearly melts when she sees the hope in his eyes.

"OK, yes," she says. "It's a date."

Chapter 14

SAWYER STUMBLES CLUMSILY THROUGH THE REST of the week as she adjusts to balancing motherhood and her career. Paul is busy getting settled in at Morgan Stanley, so she doesn't talk to him at all other than their daily exchange of playful texts. By the time Saturday rolls around, she's a bundle of nerves and excitement.

Ava and Mike come over late that morning, and Mike stays with Matthew as Sawyer and Ava slip out to a local boutique to find Sawyer a new outfit to wear for the date. They settle on a green floral sundress that Sawyer never would have chosen for herself, but that makes her feel beautiful as soon as she puts it on. Then Ava insists on taking her to a lingerie shop "just in case."

"You *cannot* let Paul see you in your granny panties!" she declares.

"Relax—Paul is not going to see me in anything other than this dress," Sawyer says.

"Yeah, yeah," Ava replies, rolling her eyes.

But Sawyer buys a new black bra and matching silk underwear, and when she slips into them at 4:15, she feels more exhilarated than she has in a long time. She feels *alive*.

She pulls on the green dress, then sits down at her vanity and begins to put on makeup. She figures Paul is on the way already. Although he lives on the Upper West Side of Manhattan and Sawyer offered to meet him in the city, he insisted on driving to Ridgewood to pick her up. He said he'd be there around 5 o'clock. Ava hadn't stopped raving about his silver BMW, which he apparently pays over $400 per month to park in a garage two blocks from his apartment building. Sawyer can't imagine paying that much money just to park a car. But, as she knows from her best friend's huge house and pricey vacations, investment banking pays well.

Sawyer is just about ready when she hears the doorbell ring at 4:53. A jolt of adrenaline runs through her, and she looks around maniacally for her purse. She hears a hum of voices as Ava or Mike opens the door and lets Paul in.

Sawyer spots her purse on the corner of her bed and double checks to make sure she has everything she needs. She grabs her cell phone from the vanity and then slips on the white wedge sandals she pulled out of her closet. She takes one last look in the mirror, noting how great the green dress complements her dark wavy hair. *I clean up pretty well*, she thinks. Then she takes a deep breath, opens her bedroom door and walks down the short hallway to the living room.

Her heart stops. Paul is cradling Matthew in his arms with the baby's head resting in his left hand. He's bouncing around the room and cooing at Matthew, who's rewarding him with smiles. Ava is standing beside Mike in the corner of the room, clutching her chest as she watches the scene unfold.

Sawyer feels something stir inside of her, and she blinks back tears. "Hi," she says, "I see you've met Matthew."

Paul looks up and locks eyes with Sawyer. His eyes widen as his gaze takes her in.

"Wow," he says. "You look … absolutely stunning, Sawyer. And Matthew here is quite the little charmer."

Ava beams as she reaches out to retrieve the baby.

"Yes, my bestie and my godson are amazing!" she says. "Now get a move on, you two! Have so much fun!"

"Geez—you're kicking the girl out of her own apartment?" Mike asks playfully.

"That I am," Ava says. "And I'm kicking *you* out soon to go pick up our sushi!"

"Yes, boss," Mike replies.

Sawyer tries to take Matthew from Ava, but Ava pulls away.

"Don't even think about it!" she says. "You don't need to go out smelling like spit-up!"

So Sawyer covers her son's cheek with kisses instead. "Have fun with Auntie Ava and Uncle Mike," she tells him as he gurgles back at her. "I love you."

"OK, now go!" Ava says, and she shoves Sawyer and Paul out the door.

Chapter 15

OUTSIDE SAWYER'S APARTMENT COMPLEX, PAUL opens the passenger door of the BMW and she slides in. The black leather seats still have that new-car smell, even though Paul bought the sedan five months earlier. It's a far cry from Sawyer's used Toyota Corolla with the car seat in the back.

"Matthew really is adorable," Paul remarks as he pulls onto the road.

"He is, isn't he?" Sawyer replies with a giggle. "And you were a natural with him. You looked so comfortable holding him."

"I've had practice," Paul replies. "My younger sister, Melissa, has a 2-year-old daughter named Jasmine who's the apple of my eye. I spend most Sundays at their house on Long Island. My parents go too. We're all really close."

A family man, Sawyer thinks.

"Where do your parents live?" she asks.

"In Brooklyn, in the house I grew up in. It's small, but we never felt like we didn't have enough space. My parents were both high school teachers, and they also worked part-time jobs in the summer to give

Melissa and me a good life. And they really pushed us to work hard at school. That hard work led me to get almost a full scholarship to Fordham, which is the only way I could have afforded it. And the strong work ethic they instilled in me spurred me to work a few jobs all through college and save up to pay for business school at Fordham. I had a bunch of student loans when I graduated from there, but I was able to pay them off pretty quickly. I owe all of my success to my parents."

Sawyer is fascinated by every word Paul says. She's never quite figured out how to talk about her accomplishments without sounding like she is bragging, but somehow Paul is managing to do just that. She can tell that his story is meant to sing his parents' praises rather than his own.

"Your parents sound wonderful," she tells him. "I'm very close with my family too. I'm an only child, but I have a bunch of aunts, uncles and cousins, and Ava is like my sister. Oh, and I was going to Fordham business school as well, for marketing."

"You *were* going?" Paul asks.

"I dropped out after my first year when I found out I was pregnant," Sawyer explains. "I'm hoping to reenroll when Matthew is a bit bigger."

She wonders for a moment whether Paul will judge her for this, but he just nods his head with understanding. "That would have been a lot to handle," he tells her. "You'll have time to go back to school. And Matthew's not such a bad trade-off."

"No, he sure isn't," Sawyer says. She smiles and leans her head against the headrest. She's not sure how Paul has managed to make her feel so comfortable already, but she definitely likes it.

He takes her to Le Bernardin, a Michelin-starred restaurant a few blocks from the theater that's notoriously difficult to get a reservation.

Sawyer can't believe it. She asks how he scored a table, and he says a colleague from his former company has "connections." She suspects that Paul is actually the one with the connections, but she doesn't press him on it.

The meal is to die for, but it could be Waffle House and Sawyer would be having just as fabulous a time. The conversation flows easily, and neither Sawyer nor Paul feels the need to fill the couple of quiet moments that do arise. Sawyer is struck by how down-to-earth Paul is despite all his wealth. She can see the outline of his chiseled physique under his fitted Lacoste polo, and learns that it comes from lifting weights in his building's gym and jogging in Riverside Park rather than working out at a pricey fitness center. She discovers that he's a huge baseball fan like her—albeit a fan of the wrong team—and that he and a friend split Yankees season tickets in the 300 level, not in the fancy field-level seats. ("All the *real* fans sit up high!" he declares, and she agrees despite having never sat in field-level seats and not really knowing the difference). She learns that, like her, his ideal evening involves greasy pizza, sweatpants and Netflix.

And Sawyer finds herself opening up to Paul more than she'd expected to. She tells him about how she accidentally got pregnant and that Matthew's father had not been in the picture from the beginning. She tells him how panicked she felt at first, but how she eventually got comfortable with—and then excited about—the idea of becoming a mom.

And she talks a lot about Matthew—how he's given her a purpose in life that she didn't even realize she was missing. How even though she's made peace with being a single mother, she still sometimes feels searing stabs of loneliness. And she shares her biggest fear—that Matthew will always struggle with his identity because he'll never know his father.

All the while, Paul listens attentively. He asks all the right questions and gives her just the right words of encouragement. Sawyer feels like she can sit at that table and talk to him all night. But before she knows it, 7:30 rolls around and Paul asks for the check.

"Are you excited for the show?" he asks her.

"Oh my gosh—you have *no* idea!" Sawyer says. "I am obsessed with the *Hamilton* soundtrack, and I know all the words! I've been dying to see the show but … it just hasn't happened."

Paul's face lights up, and he admits that he, too, knows all the words to the *Hamilton* soundtrack and even owns the coffee table book about the show.

"I saw it once, a year ago, with my parents and sister," he says. "It was amazing—but I'm sure it will be even better seeing it with you."

Sawyer feels herself blush. "Thank you so much for taking me," she says. "You have no idea how much it means to me."

Paul pays the bill, and they leave the restaurant. As they walk to the theater, he grabs Sawyer's hand, and she is struck by how comfortable it feels. She's not quite sure what she did to deserve this amazing night with such a great man, but she decides to just enjoy it and not question it. *I deserve this*, she tells herself.

Chapter 16

THE SHOW IS EVERY BIT AS MAGICAL AS SAWYER EX-
pects it to be. They have seventh-row seats in the center of the orchestra
section, and Sawyer is mesmerized by everything happening on the
stage. She and Paul hold hands almost the entire time. They get a case
of the silent giggles when an old lady sitting behind them shushes them
loudly for singing along under their breaths.

When they exit the theater around 11 p.m., Sawyer is absolutely
giddy. Everything about the evening—the delicious meal and wine,
the intimate conversation, Paul's careful attention to her, and the excitement and spectacle of the show—has made her feel a certain way.
At first she can't quite put a finger on it, but then she recognizes the
feeling—she's turned on!

Gosh, it's been so long since she's been touched by a man. She
hadn't thought much about sex at all since she found out she was pregnant, but she is suddenly gripped with an overwhelming hunger to feel
Paul's hands on her body. Suddenly, an image of Ethan's blue eyes gazing into hers as he enters her flashes into her mind. A wave of anxiety
seizes her.

Don't be crazy, Sawyer, she thinks to herself. *Ethan is gone now, and Paul is the perfect man. Do not screw this up.*

They arrive at the garage, and Paul retrieves their parking ticket from his pocket. He hands it to a burly attendant, who is clearly annoyed the theater crowd has arrived to retrieve their cars, and he can no longer play Candy Crush Saga on his phone.

"Be right back," he grunts, and disappears into the garage to get the BMW.

Paul turns to Sawyer. "What's wrong?"

Sawyer is struck by how perceptive he is, and she wonders how direct she should be. But then she thinks about how honest he has been with her since the moment they met and how much she has already opened up to him. She realizes how much she already trusts him.

"Well," she says. "Nothing is *wrong.* I'm just thinking about what a great night it's been and how much I'd love to come back to your apartment with you."

Paul raises one eyebrow. "Wow," he says. "That is absolutely *not* what I was expecting to hear."

Sawyer giggles. "I'm just full of surprises," she coos.

Paul sighs and looks down at his feet. "I agree about tonight— it was perfect in every way. And I'd absolutely love to see you again. But—and I can't believe I'm saying this— I don't want to tarnish the evening by taking advantage of you."

Now it's Sawyer's eyebrows that shoot up, and she feels her cheeks begin to get hot.

"Take advantage of me?" she asks. "I'm not even the slightest bit tipsy, Paul. Whatever wine we drank at dinner wore off during the show. I know exactly what I'm doing … and what I'd *like* to be doing."

He places his hand on her cheek. "That's not what I mean, Sawyer," he says. "It's just that I know it's been a long time since you've … been with somebody. And I don't want you to do anything you may regret tomorrow morning."

"I'm not going to regret it," Sawyer insists.

He moves his hand from her cheek and places his finger on her lips.

"Shhh," he whispers. "There's no rush, Sawyer. You know where I stand. I'm looking for something serious, and I *really* like you. I think we can have something very special. So I'm not planning on going anywhere, and I hope you're not, either."

"I'm not," she replies softly.

"Good. Then maybe I can convince you to come to a Yankees game next Saturday. They're playing the Mets—it's the Subway Series. And if we can get through that without killing each other, we can get through anything."

She giggles. "I'll see what I can do about a babysitter."

"OK," he says. And then he leans down and gives her the softest, most tender kiss. She kisses him back, and she's about to wrap her arms around him when she hears the grunt of Burly Attendant Guy.

"Hell*o*!" he says. "Your car—it's here!"

He motions at the BMW and then tosses the keys to Paul. Sawyer and Paul lock eyes and burst into laughter. Then they hop into the BMW and drive off.

Chapter 17

"SAWYER, THE TABLE IS CLEARED OFF," PAUL SAYS, ducking his head into Sawyer's parents' kitchen. "I'm just gonna take these bags of trash out and then we can do birthday cake."

"Thanks, babe," Sawyer replies as she rummages through the junk drawer. "Now where the heck did I put those candles?"

Ava looks up from the kitchen table, where she's arranging tiny plastic Elmo figurines on top of Matthew's first birthday cake. "I'm telling you, Seesaw. That man is a gem," she says.

Sawyer nods. "I know, Ava. You don't have to keep reminding me."

"I'm pretty sure I do, though," Ava says as she steps back to get a better look at the cake. Satisfied with her arrangement of Elmos, she turns to the sink to wash her hands. "The man asked you to move in with him and you said, 'I'll think about it.' *Really*, Seesaw? You'll *think* about it? What's there to think about?"

"*Here* they are!" Sawyer says triumphantly as she finds the candles.

"I know you heard me," Ava presses.

Sawyer sighs. "I heard you loud and clear, Ava. But it's not like he's asking me to move in with him down the street, or even in New York. He wants me to move to Scarsdale! *Westchester!*"

"Oh, I feel *so* bad for you," Ava says, her voice dripping with sarcasm. "Your rich and handsome boyfriend, who also happens to be one of the nicest people on the planet, wants to move you and your son into a mansion in Scarsdale so he can be the vice president of an investment firm in Westchester and get even richer. You poor, poor thing."

"What about my parents? And you and Mike? And my *job*?" Sawyer replies.

"Oh, please. Scarsdale is less than an hour away from here. It's not like it's across the country. You're making excuses because you're afraid. Paul is the perfect guy and this is everything you've ever wanted, and you know it."

Sawyer sighs but does not respond. Ava is right—after nine months of dating Paul, she can honestly say he checks all the boxes. He is completely devoted to her and Matthew—you'd never know he wasn't Matthew's biological father—and her parents adore him. He is unbelievably handsome, yet down-to-earth, and she'd never have to worry about money again. He is kind to waiters, he looks people in the eye when he talks to them and he makes her laugh. Most importantly, he is ready to buy a home and settle down with her and Matthew. After spending her entire dating life seeking this very situation, Sawyer finally has it.

And yet, something has been nagging at her—something she'd never admit to anyone, not even Ava. For almost the entire time she's been with Paul, Ethan will suddenly pop into her head without warning. And when he does, her entire body comes alive as if it's pulsing with electrical currents. She'll find herself consumed with yearning for him, obsessing over where he is and what he's doing. Is he happy? Has he found another woman? Does he ever think about her?

It's unbelievable, really, how a man she spent one night with could have such a hold on her. But even in that short time, Sawyer had felt a connection with Ethan that she's never quite felt with Paul, or with any man for that matter. Though Paul knows all the day-to-day details about her life—what her hair looks like when she wakes up in the morning (Bedhead Central), how she likes her Dunkin' Donuts coffee (large hazelnut, three milks, two sugars), her real favorite TV show (*Supermarket Sweep*) and not the one she tells people is her favorite (*Manifest*)—she feels like Ethan had gotten to know the *essence* of her. Part of it was because she expected him to be a one-night stand and therefore felt no pressure, she opened up to him in a way she never had with any other man. She shared her insecurities with him. She told him about things she'd done that she wasn't proud of. She even admitted to him that when Ava called her after Mike proposed, she hung up and wept into her pillow for 10 minutes rather than feel happy because she'd been so consumed with jealousy.

The other part, though, is something Sawyer can't quite put her finger on. It's just this overwhelming sense that Ethan naturally understood her, even without her needing to say anything at all. Like when he looked into her eyes, he really *saw* her. It's crazy, she knows. It is something she believed only existed in the movies. But she can't deny the familiarity that had been there from the very first minute they'd met in the gazebo.

And it wasn't one-sided. Ethan had been completely vulnerable with Sawyer as well. He cried when he told her about his dad leaving when he was 8. How after his mom remarried two years later and had his half-brother and sister, he never quite felt like he fit in with the family.

That he still often felt like he didn't fit in with the world. He really let Sawyer in and gave her the kind of connection she always craved.

With Paul, Sawyer knows all the important details. She knows his favorite beer (Blue Moon), his proudest accomplishment (running the Boston Marathon) and his worst habit (sleepwalking into the kitchen in the middle of the night and eating Chips Ahoy! cookies). But she feels like she'll never truly know his essence the way she did Ethan's. She knows Paul will never be completely vulnerable with her, that he'll always have just a little bit of a wall up. And it isn't because he doesn't trust her. It's just his nature. He'd been raised to be strong and levelheaded—to focus on working hard and moving forward rather than letting things bring him down. He takes amazing care of her and Matthew—both emotionally and physically—but he's never given her the opportunity to take care of him. He's never made her feel like he *needs* her—and to Paul, that is the way life should be. He is a man who takes pride in helping others and in caring for his loved ones, without needing to be cared for himself. But Sawyer *wants* to take care of him. She wants to peel back every layer of him, to see all his cracks and blemishes. But she knows he'll never let her.

Still, Sawyer does love and appreciate Paul. Their life together is stable, comfortable and fun, and she knows how lucky she is to have found him. She also knows what a great father figure he is to Matthew. He does it all—changes diapers, sings along to Parachute Express songs on Alexa, reads board books at bedtime.

But it's those unexpected moments that jar her—the ones where Ethan suddenly seems to be right there with her. Like when she and Paul are making love. Sex with Paul is like every other aspect of their relationship—comfortable and dependable. He had learned early on exactly where to touch her to make her orgasm quickly. But sometimes, they'll be right in the middle of it, and Sawyer will suddenly remember Ethan's eyes and hands hungrily exploring every inch of her body, as if he wanted to memorize every freckle and line.

Sometimes, she'll be at yet another amazing restaurant with Paul and have a flashback to being at the speakeasy with Ethan. She'll remember how utterly alive she felt when she looked into those blue eyes across the table and saw right into Ethan's soul.

Sometimes, she'll be playing with Paul and Matthew on the floor, and Matthew will giggle in a way that reminds her of Ethan's laugh. She'll imagine Ethan making silly faces and knocking down the block tower, then scooping Matthew up and hugging him with the same intensity with which he'd held her during their one night together.

These moments always throw Sawyer off for a bit. Sometimes the uneasiness lasts hours, sometimes days, but it always passes. Sawyer assuages her guilt by telling herself that she only thinks about Ethan so much because he is the father of her baby, and she never got closure with him. She remembers all her failed relationships and how secure she feels with Paul and how fortunate she is. And she notes how easily Paul fits in with her family and with Ava and Mike. And then she picks herself back up and forges on with life.

Like right now. Sawyer looks at Ava and says, "Ready?" Then she picks up the cake and heads out onto the deck to sing happy birthday to her son.

Chapter 18

MATTHEW IS EQUALLY CONFUSED AND DELIGHTED as the small group of friends and family sings to him. Sawyer blows out the candles, then stands next to Paul behind Matthew's highchair as her mom, Paul's mom and sister, and Ava all try to get a picture of the trio.

"Matthew, sweetie! Look at Gwandma!" Mrs. Reynolds coos.

"Matthew! Look who Auntie Melissa has!" Paul's sister calls, waving the baby's beloved stuffed Elmo over her head.

When the doting aunts and grandmas are satisfied with their photos, Sawyer cuts the cake and passes slices to everyone. Matthew gets the first piece—his first taste of cake ever—and goes absolutely nuts, digging into it with his hands and shoving fistfuls into his mouth. By the time he's finished, blue frosting covers his face, and he's forced to sit for another round of photos as he tries to wrestle his way out of the highchair.

"Well, we'd better get him upstairs for a bath," Sawyer says once the snapping stops. She unstraps him and picks him up.

"Actually," Paul says, smiling at Sawyer. "Why don't you let your mom hold Matthew for a minute while I do something?"

Sawyer looks over at her mother, who's already yanking Matthew from her arms. "What's going on?" Sawyer asks her.

Her mother doesn't answer and instead exchanges a knowing glance with her dad.

Sawyer turns to the rest of the family. Ava's clasping her hands with excitement. Mike is looking away and pretending not to see what's happening. Melissa, her husband and Paul's parents are beaming. Only little Jasmine seems as confused as Sawyer.

"*What* is going *on*?" Sawyer asks again, louder.

Paul steps in front of Sawyer and grabs both of her hands. "Look at me, sweetheart," he tells her.

Sawyer looks into his brown eyes and is struck by the overwhelming amount of love pouring out of them. That cozy feeling of warmth and safety washes over her. And that's when she realizes what is happening. Her heart begins to race.

"Sawyer, meeting you and Matthew was a dream come true for me," Paul says. "You two have given me something that was missing from my life. Something I've wanted for a very long time—a family."

"Oh my God," Sawyer gasps as a tear escapes her right eye and rolls down her cheek.

"You two have made me feel complete, and I love you both more than I could have ever imagined. I can't picture my life without you in it."

Paul reaches into his pocket, pulls out a turquoise Tiffany box and drops to one knee. Ava squeals as she tries and fails to fight back the tears that begin to gush down her face. Paul opens the box, revealing a 6-carat cushion-cut diamond that's exactly what Sawyer would have chosen for herself.

"Sawyer, will you please make me the luckiest, happiest, richest man alive and marry me?"

In that moment, Sawyer doesn't think of Ethan. She doesn't think of anything except the amazing man earnestly looking up at her and all the surrounding people who love him as much as she does—especially Matthew. A feeling of peace washes over her.

"Yes," she tells him. "Absolutely—yes."

Paul's face explodes with joy. He slips the ring onto Sawyer's finger—it fits just slightly loose—then stands and envelops her in a hug as their family and friends whoop and clap. Mrs. Reynolds brings Matthew over and hands him to Paul, who holds him in the crook of his right arm while keeping his left arm around Sawyer. Cameras click all around them as Sawyer clutches Paul and Matthew.

You did good, Sawyer, she thinks to herself. *Everything will be OK from now on.*

Chapter 19

THE NEXT YEAR FLIES BY IN A WHIRLWIND OF EX-
citement and a flurry of activity. Sawyer barely has a moment to think,
let alone think about Ethan.

Immediately after the proposal, Sawyer and Paul begin house hunt-
ing in Scarsdale. Paul wants her to have her dream house, but he also
doesn't want the process to take too long—his new job at an investment firm in Valhalla begins in two months. Luckily, Scarsdale has
no shortage of dream homes, and they find the perfect one only three
weeks later. It's a brick two-story home with stately columns flanking
the entrance, a circular driveway and a huge backyard for Matthew to
play in. Its 4,300 square feet includes five bedrooms, four bathrooms
and a finished basement. Sawyer can hardly believe it's hers.

The next thing she does is quit her job. She's less torn about it than
she thought she'd be. Setting up the house, planning the wedding and
caring for Matthew will keep her plenty busy, and the commute would
be harrowing. And with her lack of a graduate degree preventing a promotion, she's started to get bored with her job, anyway.

They get married the following June, two months after Matthew's second birthday. It's the fairy tale wedding Sawyer had always dreamed of, at Oheka Castle on Long Island. Jasmine and Matthew serve as the flower girl and ring bearer, and the guests laugh and coo as Jasmine yanks a toddling Matthew down the aisle. When Sawyer herself walks down the aisle on her father's arm and sees the way Paul looks at her in her ivory mermaid gown, she feels so safe and loved—like her life has finally become what she's always wanted it to be.

She and Paul honeymoon in Bora Bora for 10 days while their parents take turns watching Matthew. It's quite magical. They have their own private bungalow above the turquoise lagoon, with a glass floor in the living room through which they watch tropical fish and stingrays swim by. They take an open-air Jeep tour through the mountains, sip fruity drinks on the beach and spend a day at the resort's spa, where they get a couple's massage and lounge in hot tubs.

They meet a bunch of younger honeymooners at breakfast and at the pool, some of whom complain about the lack of nighttime entertainment. But that's not much of a problem for Sawyer and Paul, neither of whom can manage to keep their eyes open past 9 p.m. Early one morning toward the end of the trip, as Sawyer looks out at the lagoon while Paul snores next to her in bed, she wonders if all the other honeymooners are having way more sex than she and Paul are. They'd only done it twice on the trip—they'd been smoked after full days of eating and drinking in the sun—and both times had been predictably pleasant. But Sawyer wonders if there's something wrong with them, and that fills her with anxiety. Shouldn't they feel more passion for each other? Shouldn't they want each other more? Shouldn't the sight of Sawyer in her bikini make Paul want to jump her bones?

But then she tells herself she's being ridiculous. She and Paul are in their 30s, with a 2-year-old child. Paul gets to work at 7 a.m. every morning so he can be home by 5:30. Add to that all the big events of the past year, and it's no wonder they're both exhausted.

Besides, she loves Paul, and he loves her. They're a family, and they've already built such a beautiful life together. That's way more important than sex or passion or butterflies. Right at that moment, Paul rolls over and greets her with sleepy eyes.

"Morning, beautiful," he says.

"Good, you're up," she tells him. "I'm starving."

They go to breakfast and spend the rest of the day lounging on their bungalow's private deck, reading books (a Harry Truman biography for him, an Elin Hilderbrand beach read for her) and jumping into the water to snorkel and swim in between.

When the trip ends two days later, Sawyer already feels the post-vacation blues as she takes one last look at the floating bungalow. But when she gets off the plane at LaGuardia Airport and finds her parents and Matthew waiting for them at baggage claim, she bursts into tears of joy. She missed her boy so much, and wrapping her arms around him again fills her with contentment and relief.

Things get even better two months later when Paul officially adopts Matthew as his son. They go out to dinner with both their families and Ava and Mike to celebrate, during which they record countless videos of Matthew calling Paul "Daddy."

When they go to bed that night, Sawyer is overwhelmed with hope for the future. She had so enjoyed the blur of house decorating and wedding planning over the past year. But now that they'd made the house their own, the wedding was over and thank-you cards were sent, and Paul had settled into his career, real life is about to begin—and Sawyer is ready for it.

Chapter 20

February, two years and 8 months later

SAWYER TAKES ONE LAST GLANCE IN THE BEDROOM mirror and sighs. A few years ago, she would have never dreamed of going out for brunch looking like this. She thought she'd have more time to get ready after her workout, but as soon as she got home from dropping Matthew off at preschool, she'd seen his Paw Patrol lunchbox sitting on the kitchen island. Cursing under her breath, she grabbed it and rushed right back out the door to bring it to the school. That had wasted nearly 30 minutes.

When she got home, she'd decided to hop on the treadmill for half an hour, but on her way past the laundry room she remembered the load of laundry that had been sitting in the washer since yesterday morning. She opened the washer, sniffed the wet clothes and decided it wasn't worth re-washing them. So, she shoved as much as she could into the dryer and hung all of her and Matthew's cotton tees on the drying rack. By that time, she only had 20 minutes left for her run. But on her way down to the basement gym, her cell phone rang and Paul's work number flashed on the screen.

"Hey," she said breathlessly as she raced down the stairs.

"Hey!" Paul replied in a relaxed voice. "How's your morning going?"

"Same as it always goes," Sawyer snapped, not meaning to sound as annoyed as she felt. "How's yours?"

"I met some clients for breakfast in White Plains, which is why I left so early this morning, he replied. "Now I'm back in the office and getting ready for a meeting."

Sawyer rolled her eyes. How would she know he left early that morning? Paul was always gone before she even woke up on weekdays. He usually came home between 5:30 and 6 p.m., by which time she was exhausted from shuttling Matthew around town and doing freelance marketing work for her former company. Paul would always stroll in looking as handsome and put-together as ever in his designer suit, while Sawyer often hadn't even showered yet.

Granted, Paul would jump right into playing with Matthew, which would often allow Sawyer to take an evening workout class or get some more work done. Still, she was finding it harder and harder not to resent Paul. She missed working full time and her Margarita Mondays with Ava. She missed adult conversation. She missed wearing nice clothes. She even missed riding the bus.

"Good! Let me run. I'm meeting Ava for brunch in an hour, and I really wanted to hop on the treadmill real quick. I haven't seen her in a month, so I don't want to be late."

"Everything OK?" Paul asked, concern in his voice.

"Fine," Sawyer replied. "I'm just in a hurry. I'll see you later."

"OK ... love you."

"Love you, too." And she hung up.

By that point, Sawyer knew she should have given up on the workout, but it had been a few days since she'd been able to fit one in. So she did a quick 15 minutes on the treadmill, took the fastest shower ever and threw on maroon yoga pants and a long navy hoodie that she knew didn't match.

She takes one last sad glance in the mirror and catches the time on her Apple Watch as she twists her hair into a messy topknot.

"Shit, I gotta go!" she says aloud.

She runs downstairs, grabs her keys from the kitchen island and rushes out the door. She doesn't realize she left her purse at home until she parks her car in downtown Scarsdale, already 10 minutes late for brunch.

Chapter 21

SAWYER RUSHES THROUGH THE FRONT DOOR OF HER favorite café and immediately spots Ava sipping a mimosa at a table along the left wall. She's wearing a fitted black turtleneck, ripped skinny jeans and knotted leopard-print headband. Her makeup, as usual, looks flawless.

Sawyer slides breathlessly into the seat across from her. "Hey, bestie," she says.

Ava looks up from her iPhone and breaks into a wide smile. "*Hey*!" she says. "No coat? Aren't you cold? It's freezing out there!"

Sawyer sighs. "I'm lucky I remembered to put a shirt on this morning. I'm parked just down the street—no worries."

"As long as you put a coat on that nephew of mine!" Ava replies.

"Yes, *Mom*," Sawyer says. "And while we're nagging, should *you* be drinking a mimosa?"

"Relax—it's just orange juice. I asked the waitress to put it in a Champagne glass so I can feel festive."

"That's my girl," says Sawyer. "And you look amazing, as always."

"So do you!"

"No I don't, and you know it."

Ava sighs. "Fine—you look exactly like you're supposed to look—like a busy mom. And frankly, I can't wait to look like that in six months' time!"

Right on cue, Sawyer yawns. She is over the moon for Ava and Mike, who finally got pregnant after a year of fertility treatments and had just entered the second trimester. But right now, she's starving, frazzled and just plain grouchy.

"We'll see if you feel the same way when the time comes," she jokes.

A young, perky blonde waitress appears. Sawyer doesn't recognize her, so she must be new. "Are you ladies ready to order?" the waitress asks.

"Absolutely. I'll have the Greek omelet and the strongest cup of coffee you can muster, please," Sawyer says.

"We only make our coffee one strength, I think," the waitress replies.

Ava catches Sawyer's eye and tries her hardest to stifle a laugh. But Sawyer is too tired to even crack a smile, so she just says, "Any coffee will do, then."

The waitress scribbles the order down on her notepad and turns to Ava. "And for you?"

"I'll have the same, minus the strongest cup of coffee you can muster."

The waitress opens her mouth as if to correct Ava, but then changes her mind and nods. "All right, then—I'll get those omelets to you right away."

"And the coffee!" Sawyer calls as the waitress walks away. She turns back to Ava. "My God. Guess you don't need to be smart to work here."

Ava shakes her head. "Geez, Sawyer—lighten up. What the heck has gotten into you?"

Sawyer sighs. She had promised herself that she wouldn't use this brunch to vent. She didn't want to take away from Ava's excitement about her pregnancy or have Ava think *she* wasn't excited about the baby. But being in the safety of her best friend's company unleashes a wave of emotions she's been bottling in for—how long now? She can't even remember.

"I don't know, Ava. Everything. Everything is bothering me."

Ava's eyebrows shoot up with surprise. "Talk to me, Seesaw. Tell me what's wrong."

And for the next 15 minutes or so, Sawyer does just that. She talks about being in a perpetual state of stress, jumping from one task to the next without any transition time. Feeling like she's never fully in the moment because her mind is always thinking about the next thing on her to-do list. That even the "fun" things she used to enjoy doing with Matthew—things like bringing him on playdates and doing arts and crafts—have started to feel like just another chore. And then she says aloud the thing she is most ashamed of.

"And my marriage—not even *that* makes me happy anymore," she says. Tears begin rolling down her cheeks.

The perky blonde waitress appears with two plates of food. She glances uncomfortably at Sawyer and practically sprints away from the table after laying the plates down.

"My God, Sawyer. How long have you been feeling this way?"

"I don't really know. I think it's been building up over the past year."

"Why didn't you tell me?"

Sawyer shrugs. "I don't know. It was never as bad as it's been over the past few months. And we've been so happy about the baby that I didn't want to put a damper on it."

Ava takes a bite of her omelet and closes her eyes. "*Yum!*"

"I know," Sawyer says, stabbing a fork in her own omelet. "It's my favorite."

They eat quietly for a few minutes as Ava tries to absorb everything her best friend just told her. Then she sighs and looks at Sawyer. "Do you still love Paul?"

"Of course I do, Ava," Sawyer replies. "I can't imagine my life without him. It's just that I feel … unfulfilled. Like something is missing, I guess."

Something flashes across Ava's face that makes Sawyer instantly regret what she just said.

"*What's* missing, Sawyer? You have everything you've ever wanted. You have this incredible man who adores you and would do anything for you. You have a gorgeous house. You work part time on your own hours so you can be with your perfect child, who by the way, you didn't even have to *try* to have …"

"I know, I know," Sawyer interrupts. "I'm so sorry, Ava. I know how much you and Mike went through for your baby. I know I sound ungrateful, but I'm not. I'm *so* grateful for everything I have. But don't you see? That's part of the problem. I know I have no reason to feel this way, and yet I still do. And I can't figure out why. The guilt and shame are so unbearable sometimes. It's crushing. But I can't help how I feel. Believe me, I'd give anything not to feel this way."

Ava remains quiet and continues to eat. Finally, she sighs.

"I know you can't help how you feel, Seesaw. And I shouldn't have invalidated your feelings just because of my situation. I'm sorry for that. But please, help me understand. What could possibly be missing from your life?"

Sawyer shakes her head. "I don't know, Ava. I've been trying to put my finger on it for a while now, but I just can't figure out what it is. One thing I can say, though, is that I've really been missing going to work every day."

"You don't even *have* to work, Seesaw," Ava says. "You could never work another day in your life and still never have to worry about money."

"That doesn't mean I don't *want* to work," Sawyer replies.

"But you're always complaining about your deadlines and not being able to juggle everything as it is."

"I know, and that's because I'm trying to do two things—be a stay-at-home mom *and* be a working mom. Sometimes I feel like it would be easier to just be at an office all day."

"So why don't you?"

"Same reasons you're planning to quit," Sawyer replies. "Because I never wanted to hire a nanny for Matthew, and I didn't want to put him in preschool full time. I wanted to be with him while he was little."

"Well, he's starting kindergarten in September. Maybe you can think about getting a full-time job then."

"Actually … I was thinking about finishing my master's degree. I looked into it, and I can transfer my credits to Manhattanville College. I can finish my degree there. Classes would be a couple nights per week, and I wouldn't have to drive all the way into the city."

"That's great!" Ava says. "What does Paul think?"

"I haven't told him yet," Sawyer replies. "But I have to get my application in soon, so I'll talk to him about it before then."

"And he will totally support you. You know he just wants you to be happy."

"I know," Sawyer says. "And then once I finish my degree next year, maybe I can go back to my company and head a department like I wanted to. Or maybe find a job somewhere closer. We'll see."

Ava places her balled-up napkin on her plate and pushes it aside. "Well, this all sounds like it's going to be the answer, and that should make you feel better already. I feel like once you go back to school, you'll find what's been missing."

Sawyer sighs. "School will definitely help. But it's not going to magically make everything amazing with Paul."

Ava rolls her eyes. "Why not, Sawyer? What's so bad about your marriage?"

"It's not *bad*," Sawyer replies. "I told you, I love Paul. He's a great dad. We have a great life. We have fun together. It's just … I don't know. There's no passion."

Ava laughs. "What did you think? Did you think you'd be married with a kid and still be having mind-blowing, passionate sex?"

"I thought I'd still be *having* sex, period," Sawyer replies. "We're both so tired and busy that it hardly ever happens anymore. And besides, it was never mind-blowing with Paul."

"Well, that's common when you have young kids. And you don't marry someone for the mind-blowing sex," Ava declares. "You marry them because they're kind, and they share your interests and they make you laugh. Because you love them, and they love you. And you have that with Paul. Don't take this the wrong way, Seesaw, but you *know* how lucky you were to meet someone so great who wanted to be with you even though you had a little baby, and who ended up loving that baby so much that he made him his own. Don't take that for granted. Please."

Sawyer is about to respond when Perky Blonde tentatively sidles back up to the table. "You ladies finished?" she asks.

Sawyer dabs at her eyes with her napkin. "We are. And I'll take the check, please."

She turns to Ava. "Are you in a hurry to get back home?"

"No way! I had the day off. Plus, I didn't drive here just to see you for brunch and go right back home. I figured we could go back to your house for a bit and then I could go with you to pick up Matthew at school and take him somewhere fun."

"Heck yeah!" Sawyer replies. "And you should stay for dinner. I know Paul would love to see you too. And that will give us plenty of time to talk about what you want me to do for your baby shower."

Ava's face lights up. "Sounds like a plan!"

Sawyer pays the bill, and she and Ava walk to their cars. As she drives home, she glances through the rearview mirror at her best friend following behind her. And just like that, she feels just a little back to normal again.

Chapter 22

Six months later

AVA IS JUST WALKING OUT THE FRONT DOOR WHEN Paul pulls into the driveway in the BMW. He jumps out of the car and rushes over to Sawyer.

"Baby! I made it!" he says breathlessly, pecking her on the lips.

"Yeah, just barely," Sawyer replies. Despite her tone, she doesn't feel annoyed with him at all. She has too much adrenaline coursing through her veins—too much to be excited about.

Everything seemed to be happening at once. Three days earlier, Sawyer had witnessed Ava and Mike's son, Nate, come into the world. She couldn't believe it when Ava asked her to be in the delivery room with her and Mike when the time came. She assumed Ava would only want Mike there, or at least her mother and Mike. But Ava looked at her like she was crazy and said "of *course*" she wanted Sawyer there.

"I was there for you when you gave birth! Why would you think I wouldn't want you to be there for me?"

The baby was 8 pounds, 4 ounces, with a full head of dark hair. He was absolutely perfect. When she held him, Sawyer felt a small pang of longing. She and Paul had talked about having another baby a few times over the years, but they were so busy that they'd never gone out of their way to make that happen. And Paul always said that as far as he was concerned, Matthew was *his* child, so he would be totally fine with not having a biological one.

But meeting Nate reminded Sawyer of her longtime dream of having a bigger family, and she knows Matthew would be an amazing big brother. Except now, Sawyer has something else to focus on—finishing grad school. Sawyer had been accepted into Manhattanville College to get her Master of Science in Marketing Communication Management, and she was able to transfer over most of her credits from Fordham. Paul, of course, fully supported the idea from the start.

"This is wonderful news!" he said, genuinely thrilled for her. "We'll do what we have to do to make it work."

When she relayed their conversation to her parents, they gushed about what an amazing, supportive man Paul was. That, of course, had caused Sawyer to feel even more guilty about the way she'd been feeling.

But today, she feels nothing but excitement. Today, she's just glad Paul made it home in time to come with her to the bus stop to pick up Matthew after his first day of kindergarten, which also happens to be *her* first day of grad school. She plans to finish cooking Matthew's favorite meal when they get home (spaghetti and meatballs), then have dinner with her boys before heading to campus early to be sure she finds where she needs to go.

"You look beautiful," Paul tells her as they walk the two blocks to the bus stop.

"You say that every day," Sawyer replies.

"But today you look extra beautiful."

"Yeah, because today I'm actually wearing *real* clothes," Sawyer says.

She felt like a kid again when she'd gone to the mall to pick out new school clothes. She figured a lot of her classmates would be attending class after work and would therefore be dressed nicely, and she wanted to fit in with them and look professional. For her first class this evening, she selected straight-leg black pants, a pink floral blouse and black leather flats.

"You better hope no one spills spaghetti sauce on your *real* clothes," Paul says, and she playfully punches him in the arm.

They arrive at the bus stop and exchange hellos with the other parents, who are all chatting. Sawyer and Paul are the only ones with a kindergartener.

"Oh, I remember when Corey and I both came to the bus stop on the first day of school," Angie Braun, the mom of a first-grader who lives two houses down, says wistfully. "Jackson was so excited to see us when he got off the bus. Now he barely notices I'm here!"

The yellow school bus pulls up two minutes later, and Sawyer feels her heart begin to race. She'd been so busy preparing for grad school all day, she hadn't realized just how much she missed Matthew.

The bus stops and the door opens. "Kindergarteners first!" the jovial bus driver calls.

Sawyer sees an older boy step out of the way, then some shuffling, and then there he is—her little blond-haired, blue-eyed boy—clunking down the steps wearing the green dinosaur backpack that's practically bigger than him.

"Mommy! Daddy!" he calls and runs into their arms as the rest of the parents ooh and aah. Paul scoops up Matthew, the backpack bouncing against his arm as they walk home.

"How was your first day, buddy?" he asks.

"It was *great*!" Matthew replies, and proceeds to relay every detail of his day. "My teacher is so nice, and I made two new friends, Gianna and Tommy, and they like Pokémon too, and the cafeteria is *so big*, and we had art class and drew a picture of our families, and Ms. Green said mine was so good, and then she hung all of our pictures up."

"Wow, buddy, that's great!" Paul says. "I'm so glad you had a good day!"

Sawyer blinks back tears. "I'm so happy you like school, baby. I hope to get to see your drawing soon!"

"You will. Ms. Green said she changes the artwork once a week and sends the old ones home. You'll love my picture. Gianna loves it too. She asked me why I have blond hair, and my mommy and daddy have brown hair. She's so silly. I told her kids can have different hair color than their mommies and daddies!"

Sawyer and Paul exchange a glance. They had just recently discussed the matter of when they should tell Matthew that Paul was not his biological dad, but they had agreed that he was still too young to fully grasp the concept. If Matthew's comment bothers Paul, he doesn't show it.

"We're home!" Paul announces as they walk up the three steps to their front porch. "Let's get your hands washed up right away, and then we can have a snack."

"But not too big of a snack!" Sawyer says. "We're going to have dinner very soon so Mommy can get to *my* school this evening. It's my first day, too!"

"Wow!" Matthew replies. "I wonder what you're gonna make in art class!"

Sawyer chuckles. "I don't think I'm going to have art class, sweetie."

"No art class? What kind of school is *that*?" Matthew asks incredulously, and Sawyer and Paul crack up. Gosh, they'd raised such an awesome kid.

The family enjoys their spaghetti dinner, and Sawyer manages to keep her blouse clean, but Matthew's shirt is spattered with sauce by the end of the meal. Sawyer offers to give him a quick bath before she leaves for school, but Paul insists he will do it after she leaves. So they play two rounds of Zingo!, Matthew's favorite game, and Matthew mysteriously wins both of them.

"I'm the *best*!" he declares.

"You sure are, buddy!" Sawyer agrees. She stands up, her heart beginning to pound. "Well, Mommy had better get going now. Have a good evening with Daddy, OK?"

"OK, Mommy," Matthew replies, reaching up to give her a hug and kiss. She inhales the scent of his hair and feels warmth rush over her body.

Paul follows Sawyer to the foyer as she begins to pull on her sweater and shoes. "I'm proud of you, sweetheart. Are you excited?"

She looks up at him. "Yeah—excited and nervous," she says.

He nods. "I know—but you'll do great."

She picks up her leather tote bag, which is now doubling as her purse, and begins to shuffle through it anxiously.

"Shit, where are my keys?" she asks, and starts to pat furiously at her pants pockets.

Paul reaches into his pocket and pulls out her key ring. "Relax—I grabbed them for you from the counter."

Sawyer sighs and takes the keys. "Thank you, babe. I'll see you around 9:30, I guess."

"OK," he replies. "Have a great first class."

"I'll try," she says. She gives him a peck on the lips and walks out the door to her car. As she pulls out of the driveway, she sees him waving to her from the window. She waves back.

He's such a good man, she reminds herself as she drives down their street.

She begins to take deep breaths in and out as she drives, trying desperately to calm her nerves. She can't understand why she feels so anxious. Sure, first-day jitters are normal, but this is beyond that. There's a feeling in the pit of her stomach that her life is about to change immeasurably.

The feeling persists as she pulls into the parking lot, as she finds her way to the building where her class will be, and as she sits in the lounge on the building's main floor, scrolling through her phone while waiting to walk to class. She feels a sharp pain in her stomach, and her right leg begins to bob up and down nervously. She imagines this is what the beginning of a panic attack feels like.

Why? she asks herself. *Why am I feeling this way? Sure, going to school will be different, but different enough to warrant a panic attack?*

Sawyer still feels slightly dizzy when she steps off the elevator 15 minutes later and makes her way down the hallway to the classroom. She wishes she'd remembered to bring a water bottle. Sawyer double-checks the number above the door matches the number on the email she was sent. When she confirms she's in the right place, she enters the large classroom and takes a seat at the far end of the fourth row (the last one), next to an attractive twentysomething Black guy in a suit who's absorbed in his laptop. A quick look around the room confirms her prediction that most of the students would be coming from work, and she's glad she bought new clothes.

Sawyer had seen from the registration email that there are 32 students in this course, and she estimates about half of them are already here. The rest trickle in over the next five minutes.

Sawyer leans down to retrieve her laptop from her tote bag, trying to calm her shaking arms. As she does, the instructor enters the room.

"Good evening, class. I'm happy to see so many of you here so early," a familiar voice says.

Sawyer freezes. *No*, she thinks to herself. *No, it can't be.*

Her arms begin to shake, and she remains bent over her bag, her heart racing. She's afraid to look up to confirm what she is thinking.

"Are you all right?" the guy sitting next to her whispers.

"Um … yes. I'm fine," Sawyer replies. She sits up. And when she sees the person standing in front of the room, she gasps. Suddenly, all her anxiety makes perfect sense. It takes all her stamina to not pass out right there.

Chapter 23

HE LOOKS THE SAME. MORE CLEAN-CUT AND DRESSED more conservatively in a navy polo shirt and khakis, but still with the same boyish good looks. His eyes are as blue as ever—she can see them clearly from the last row—and it's as if she is looking at an older version of Matthew. She freezes and wonders if the man next to her can hear her heart pounding through her chest.

"Friends, I am Ethan Porter, and I will be your instructor this semester," Ethan says, looking around the room. He doesn't seem to notice her. "Please don't call me Professor Porter or Mr. Porter. Just call me Ethan. I think you'll find that I'm a pretty easygoing guy. Hopefully I won't forget to put on shoes one evening and come to class in my flip-flops."

This elicits chuckles from the class, and Sawyer slinks further down into her seat. Her mind is racing now. She is panicking. How could she have not noticed the instructor's name? What if he sees her? She has no idea what she would say to him. But of *course* he's going to see her. It's not like this is a huge lecture with 100 students in it. And what about when he sees her name? There aren't exactly a ton of female Sawyers in the world.

Then she realizes she's being ridiculous. He probably won't even recognize her when he does see her. He probably doesn't even *remember* her. They'd spent one night together almost six years ago. He's probably happily married to some gorgeous yogini who eats only organic foods and wears long linen dresses all the time, and they have an amazing sex life.

Sawyer realizes Ethan has begun to speak again.

"Now, you're all second-year graduate students, so you know how these seminars work. They're highly interactive, and I'm going to be looking for a lot of participation and discussion based on your reading each week. Tonight, though, I'll be doing more of the talking than usual since it's the first class. Have you all finished the reading I assigned in my email last week?"

There are nods and murmurs around the room, but Sawyer stays silent. In fact, she manages to remain silent for the entire two hours of class, for two reasons. One is that Ethan does, in fact, do a large share of the talking. Two is that her seat neighbor is mercifully quiet as well and the two seats in front of them are empty, so they're able to go unnoticed for the entire class. By the time 9:00 p.m. rolls around, Sawyer's Word document is full of notes, but she feels like she hasn't really absorbed anything.

As the class packs up, her seat neighbor finally introduces himself. "I'm Kevin," he says. "I don't recognize you from last year."

"I'm Sawyer," she replies. "I wasn't here last year. I transferred my credits from a different school."

"Ah, that explains it," Kevin replies. "If I'd seen you before, I would have definitely recognized you."

Normally Sawyer would be thrilled to know that she's still got it enough to receive a compliment from a cute young guy a decade her junior, but all she can do is look over at the front of the room, where

Ethan is packing up his messenger bag. Kevin follows her gaze and rolls his eyes.

"Uh-oh—another female student drinking the Ethan Porter juice."

Sawyer feels her cheeks begin to burn, but Kevin chuckles. "Chill out—I'm just messing with you."

He stands up then, and Sawyer realizes that the other six students who'd been in their row have already filed out. She'll have to get out of there quickly if she's going to avoid Ethan. She stands up and says hurriedly, "It was nice to meet you, Kevin. I'll see you next Monday, I guess."

"See you then," he replies, and turns to leave.

Sawyer follows him, struggling to stay close behind. Just as they reach the end of the row and are about to turn to head for the door, Ethan stands up from his desk and also begins walking toward the exit.

No, Sawyer thinks. *No, no, no.*

She's practically pushing Kevin along now, actively not looking in Ethan's direction. They finally make it to the door, Sawyer staring at the floor, and Kevin steps out. She is just about to walk through as well when someone bumps into her.

"Oh, I'm sorry!" she says, flustered, even though she had been the bumpee and not the bumper. She looks up. And there, standing right in front of her, is Ethan.

They lock eyes. Sawyer is overwhelmed by the feeling that she is looking at Matthew 30 years in the future.

Ethan's eyebrows shoot up, and Sawyer can see that he does, in fact, recognize her. They both step out of the way to allow the rest of the students to leave the room, never taking their eyes off each other. Time stops. Sawyer can see Ethan's Adam's apple bob as he takes a swallow. Finally, he speaks.

"Sawyer …" he says in his low, throaty voice.

"Ethan …" she whispers back.

He hesitates, then steps forward. The next thing she knows, he is pulling her into an embrace that feels exactly the same as it had six years ago. She begins to cry. As the world fades away, Sawyer melts into the arms of the man she'd spent only one night with, but who'd been with her every second of the past six years.

Chapter 24

THEY STAND THERE HOLDING EACH OTHER FOR what feels like an eternity but is actually only about three minutes. Sawyer can feel herself shaking and Ethan's heart beating. She inhales, breathing in the scent of him, and is immediately transported back in time to Ethan's bed all those years ago. Then a vision of Paul—good, kind, loyal Paul—flashes into her mind and she knows she should pull away, but she can't. So, she waits until Ethan does.

He takes a step back and places his hands on her shoulders, drinking her in with those big blue eyes the way no other man has before—like she's a lost treasure he's spent his life searching for. She can almost see the questions in his mind as he studies her. Finally, he speaks.

"Wow ..." is all he ekes out.

She nods. "I know."

"It's been ..."

"Six years."

"Six years," he confirms. "And you haven't changed a bit."

She wonders if he can see her upper lip trembling. She wants to say something playful—*oh, I've got a few more grays*, or something like that—but instead she replies, "You haven't either."

The sound of a door closing down the hallway suddenly reminds her of where they are. "Well, I guess I'd better be …"

"Wanna go to Greta's?" he asks, referring to the 24-hour diner just off campus. "Get a bite to eat or some coffee?"

She glances down at her left wrist but realizes she left her Apple Watch at home. She slides her cell phone out of her bag to check the time and sees the screen lighting up with Paul's name. "I, um…"

Ethan takes a step back into his classroom. "It's OK, you get that. I'm gonna grab my things and lock up."

She looks at him and then back down at her phone, then takes a step away and answers the phone. "Hey," she says softly.

Paul's kind voice comes through the other end. "Hey there, Sweetie!" he says. "How was your first class?"

"It—it was great," Sawyer replies, thinking how very Paul-like it is for him to call right after class ends. "How's everything going at home?"

"Good—Matthew went down pretty quickly, and I'm just checking some emails."

Emails. Sawyer latches onto that word.

"Emails. So, you're working?"

"Yeah—Miller called right after you left and said the client that was supposed to come at 4 p.m. tomorrow decided to catch an earlier flight. So now he's coming in for an 8 a.m. meeting, and we're all scrambling to do some last-minute prep."

Sawyer knows she should feel sorry for Paul. She knows she should feel disappointed that she can't come home and have a glass of wine with him and maybe watch something on Netflix. But instead, she sees this as an opportunity. Before she has a chance to think too much, she says, "I'm gonna head down to the lounge here and look over some of the class materials for a bit. I won't be home too late."

"Why don't you just come home and do it?" Paul asks. "I'm gonna be in my office. I promise I won't bother you."

"I know you won't," Sawyer says. "But I'm pretty tired, and I'm afraid once I'm home I'll fall right asleep. I just want to get a jump on this and then I'll be home."

And since Paul has no reason not to believe her, he says, "OK— don't stay there too late. And be careful."

"I will," she replies. "I love you."

"I love you, too," he says.

And Sawyer hangs up, feeling a mix of excitement to spend time with Ethan and anxiety about how easy it had been for her to lie to Paul.

Chapter 25

TWENTY MINUTES LATER, SAWYER IS SITTING ACROSS from Ethan in a vinyl booth at Greta's, which is half full with undergrads and grad students. Ethan hasn't eaten dinner, so he orders a Greek salad and an iced tea. Sawyer quickly orders the same, both so he won't feel silly eating alone and so the waitress will leave them alone.

As soon as the waitress leaves, Ethan gets right down to business. He wasn't one to beat around the bush, a quality Sawyer found attractive.

"So … you're married," he says, nodding in the direction of her wedding band and massive engagement ring.

"I am," she says. "Over three years now. His name is Paul. How about you?"

"Me? No, I'm not married," Ethan replies, waving his hand as if the very idea of marriage is ludicrous. Sawyer feels a wave of relief, then chastises herself.

The waitress returns with the iced teas. As she walks away, anxiety washes over Sawyer. *He's going to ask if I have kids*, she thinks. But instead, he looks directly in her eyes and asks, "So what happened after we spent the night together? Why did you disappear on me?"

Sawyer is stunned by the question. She can see pain in Ethan's eyes, as if her walkout had just happened yesterday. She doesn't know what to say or how honest she should be, so she buys time by saying, "Does it really matter?"

He blanches. "Does it *matter*? Of course, it matters! We spent this incredible night together and then I woke up and you were just … gone. Like it meant nothing to you."

Sawyer feels her heart rate pick up. "Of course, it meant something to me."

"Yeah, sure it did. It meant so much that you just left."

The waitress returns with the salads, and neither Sawyer nor Ethan even looks up at her. Sawyer stares down at her plate. What can she really say?

"I'm sorry, Ethan," she says. "I panicked."

"You panicked."

She looks back at him. "Yeah, I did. I was freaked out by how strongly I felt for you after only one night. And you know what I'd gone through in the past. I was terrified of being hurt. I didn't think there was any way you felt the same about me."

His blue eyes bore holes into hers. "I did feel the same, Sawyer. To this day, it was still the most incredible night of my life."

Sawyer is speechless. She picks up her fork and begins to poke at her salad. She can't believe this. She'd convinced herself that she'd been just a one-night stand for Ethan—a particularly good one-night stand, maybe. She'd convinced herself that he didn't even give her a passing thought. And most of all, she'd convinced herself that he'd also been just a fun fling for her and that the only reason she still thought about him was Matthew.

But now, sitting across from him in that booth after all these years, she realizes just how wrong she was. This thing she had with Ethan—she could hardly call it love after only one night—was real. It *is* real. And it's lasted for six years despite the fact they haven't seen each other or spoken a single word to each other. Not even a single text message. It's lasted through her marriage to Paul and through her becoming a mother to Matthew.

Oh God, Matthew. Beautiful Matthew. Sawyer drops her fork, overcome with emotion and panic. This man across from her is Matthew's father—his biological father. And he has no idea Matthew exists. And he's been carrying a torch for her all these years.

Sawyer scoops up her purse and begins to slide across the booth. "I'm sorry, Ethan, I have to go," she says.

"No, wait—please," he replies, reaching across the table and grabbing her arm. She feels heat shoot through her entire body, a heat so strong she yanks her arm away.

"Ethan, stop," she says, glancing around the diner. "There are a lot of people from school here. You're my *professor.*"

"So? We're not doing anything. And we don't have to talk about that night if you don't want to. Just, please—let's catch up."

But Sawyer's already got her purse on her shoulder and her car key in her hand. "Ethan, I'm sorry. I just can't handle this right now, OK? You've got my number from the class roster. Call me tomorrow, any time before 3:30. That's when I …"

She pauses. She was about to say *when I pick up my son at the bus stop,* but she decides she's not ready to tell him about Matthew. She needs time to think about how she is going to handle this.

Ethan puts his hands up in defeat. "OK, Sawyer. I understand. I *will* call you tomorrow, though."

Sawyer nods and hurries out of the diner, forcing herself not to look back at Ethan. When she gets home, she gives Paul a quick kiss and tells him she's going to bed. She pops two Tylenol PMs and drifts off quickly, telling herself she'll figure out what to say to Ethan tomorrow.

Chapter 26

BUT AS IT TURNS OUT, SHE DOESN'T HAVE MUCH time to think about it. Her cell phone rings at exactly 8:30 a.m., when she's barely home from bringing Matthew to the bus. She tries to tell Ethan she'll call him back in a couple hours—she wants some time to drink her coffee, shower, gather her thoughts—but he refuses.

"Come on, talk to me. It's the least you can do for stranding me at Greta's last night," he says in his charming voice. So Sawyer brings her coffee and the Eggo waffle Matthew didn't eat out to the back deck and settles onto her favorite chaise lounge.

She finds it much easier to talk to Ethan over the phone, when she can't get lost in those blue eyes. She insists that he fill her in on his life first. After he quit his job at the golf club where Ava and Mike got married—and after Sawyer disappeared on him—he went on a yoga retreat near San Francisco to clear his head. When the people running the retreat heard about Ethan's marketing background, they told him the company was looking for a new marketing director. After one interview with the president and vice president, Ethan was hired on the spot—they said they hadn't received any applicants with his unique mix of marketing, yoga and travel experience. The job was based in San Francisco, but Ethan got to travel all around the world to the various yoga retreat sites.

"Wow—that sounds like a dream job," Sawyer says.

"In many ways, it was," Ethan acknowledges. "But after three years, I actually got tired of all the travel. I was starting to feel ready to settle down. And I realized that what I loved most about the job was not the marketing work. It was being in all the yoga studios."

"That's right—your dream was to open your own studio," Sawyer says.

"You remember that?" Ethan asks.

"Of course, I do!" says Sawyer. "I remember everything about you."

There's a pause as Ethan digests this information. Then he sighs. "Well, that dream came true, Sawyer. I found the perfect spot in Harrison. Oh man, you have to see it. It's got these gorgeous wood floors, exposed brick walls. And the best part is, I live right on top of it. How's that for a commute?"

Sawyer smiles even though Ethan can't see her. It's impossible *not* to smile, with the excitement emanating from him. She is genuinely thrilled for Ethan.

"So, what about the teaching?" Sawyer asks. "How did you end up being my professor?"

He chuckles. "Well, once I found the studio location, I had to put a lot of money into it. It was a former CrossFit gym—definitely not the vibe I was going for. So, I gutted it and basically built my dream studio from scratch. That cost a ton. And Harrison is not the cheapest place to live, as you know, so it cost a pretty penny to buy the place and the apartment upstairs. And then I had to hire instructors, front-desk people. I had to put money into advertising and building up a client base.

Somewhere in the midst of all this, a former classmate of mine who teaches in Manhattanville's marketing program decided at the last minute that she didn't want to go back after her maternity leave. This happened right before last fall's semester was about to start, and they were pretty freaked out about finding someone to take over her three classes. So, I said I'd do it while they looked for someone, but they ended up liking me, so I taught the classes all through last school year. This year, I cut down to only two classes to have more time to focus on the studio."

"And my class is one of them," Sawyer says.

"Yours is one of them."

"Wow … the world works in crazy ways."

"It sure does."

There's silence for a bit, and Sawyer notes the fact that neither of them feels the need to fill it. Finally, he asks her where she lives, and she tells him Scarsdale.

"Wow—that's like, 20 minutes from me. I've been here a year and a half, and I've never run into you."

"I looked for you, you know. After that night," Sawyer says. "I Googled you. I searched social media. I even went to your apartment, and by that point you were already gone. Some girl was living there."

"Wow … maybe you should have looked harder," Ethan says wistfully.

"I didn't know your last name!" Sawyer says. "I didn't have your phone number. And seriously, what kind of marketing guru is not on social media?"

Ethan chuckles. "I'm far from a guru, Sawyer. And you know I like to keep my personal life private. Maybe you didn't really *want* to find me."

"Maybe you didn't really want to be found," Sawyer snaps back.

"*You* disappeared on me," he replies with a tinge of impatience in his voice. "If I had thought for a second that you'd change your mind and come looking for me, I'd have set up a Facebook page in a heartbeat."

"Well, I guess it's too late now," Sawyer says.

"Too late for what?" Ethan asks. "Six years later, you walk into my classroom, and now it turns out we are practically neighbors. It's not too late for anything. It's never too late."

They talk for two more hours. Sawyer misses her Pilates class—she'll get charged a fee for skipping it without canceling. Her work goes undone. The pile of dirty laundry remains on the bedroom floor. The book she wanted to start reading on her Kindle for Ethan's class goes unread.

She fills him in on her past six years, and he listens with great interest. He asks her so many questions, especially about Paul. It's awkward, but she answers them. And then finally, she can no longer avoid the inevitable.

"So … do you and Paul want kids?" he asks her.

Her heart begins to pound. She knows she has to tell Ethan about Matthew now, and she knows she should tell him that he is Matthew's father. But the conversation had flowed so smoothly up to that point, she hadn't a chance to process everything yet—to think about how to break this monumental news to him. It was too much, too fast. So she took a deep breath and said, "We have a son. His name is Matthew. He's 5."

There's a silence that seems to stretch on forever, and Sawyer wonders if Ethan is calculating the mental math and if he is wondering whether he's Matthew's dad. But instead, he says, "Wow—congratulations, Sawyer. Why didn't you tell me until now?"

"I don't know … it just didn't come up, I guess."

"A child is a pretty big thing to just 'not come up,' " Ethan replies. "Did you think it would upset me?"

Oh God, oh God, Sawyer thinks. "I don't know—maybe," she says.

"Well, it doesn't upset me at all," Ethan replies. "I'm happy for you, Sawyer. It sounds like you have everything you've ever wanted."

"And so do you," Sawyer says. And then the air remains thick with words unspoken.

Chapter 27

"YOU DIDN'T *TELL* HIM?!" AVA HISSES THE NEXT DAY over lunch. Two old women at the next table scowl at her. Ava scowls back.

"No—I panicked!" Sawyer says. "I mean, this is all so crazy!"

"You have to tell him, Seesaw. The man has the right to know he has a child."

"And what about Paul?" Sawyer asks.

"What *about* Paul? He's always going to be Matthew's father. Ethan being back in the picture doesn't change that."

"He's not 'back in the picture,'" Sawyer retorts, but she can feel her cheeks reddening. Ava picks right up on it.

"Sawyer ..." she says in her stern mom voice, which only makes Sawyer blush even harder, confirming Ava's fears. "Sawyer, no. You listen to me. You have a beautiful life. The perfect husband who adores you. The perfect child. You are *not* going to screw this up, you hear me?"

"Relax, Ava—nothing is going to happen between me and Ethan."

"You're damn right it's not. You need to switch out of his class. *Now.*"

Sawyer sighs. "I can't, Ava. He's the only one who teaches it."

"Well, it's a conflict of interest," Ava says.

"It's not a conflict of interest. We talked about it. It's fine. We agreed that we can both be adults and that Ethan can grade me fairly. He can be impartial."

"*Impartial*?!" Ava says loudly, and their table neighbors click their tongues. "He can't be impartial, Seesaw! He's your *baby's father*!"

"All the more reason I shouldn't tell him that yet," Sawyer responds through clenched teeth. "I'm not going to do anything stupid. I'm going to see him in a classroom full of students on Monday evenings, and that's it. And then once the semester is over, I'll figure out how to tell him about Matthew. Just please don't say anything to Paul, OK?"

"So you want me to help you lie to your husband, Sawyer? Do you realize how messed up that is?"

"I'm not lying to him. I'm just not telling him I hooked up with my professor before he and I met."

"You're just not telling him that your professor is THE FATHER OF YOUR BABY!"

At this point, the old ladies' eyes look like they're going to pop out of their heads, and rather than complain about how loud Ava and Sawyer are, they now want to hear every word.

"Quiet down, Ava," Sawyer says, whispering. "Look, I know this is bad. But I need to get through this class, and that's not going to happen if I tell Paul about Ethan. So please, Ava—I don't need your judgment right now. I need your support."

Ava sighs loudly and looks away. Then she turns back to Sawyer with tears in her eyes. "I support you, Seesaw. I'll always support you. You know that. But I'm not going to support you doing anything to jeopardize your marriage to Paul. Do you hear me?"

"Loud and clear," Sawyer says. "You can trust me. I promise."

Chapter 28

THE FIRST FEW WEEKS GO BY WITHOUT INCIDENT—
Sawyer sees Ethan in class (she always sits in the back row), contributes
to class discussions while making minimal eye contact with him and
does her weekly assignments. Matthew adjusts quickly to kindergarten,
and Sawyer's fridge fills up with artwork. Paul is as supportive as ever,
holding down the fort on the two evenings Sawyer has class (Mondays
and Wednesdays). But Ava calls more frequently to "keep Sawyer in
check," and Mondays are rough—Sawyer generally spends the day in a
frenzy of nerves, trying and failing to be productive as she anticipates
seeing Ethan that evening. And as hard as she tries to fight it, Sawyer
finds herself thinking of Ethan more and more. Because of this, she
vacillates between giddiness and a nagging sense of guilt.

Paul doesn't seem to notice until the fourth Monday of Ethan's class,
while they're eating an early dinner before Sawyer has to leave. Matthew
is jabbering on about his friend Lucy at school and how she was mean
to Maddie on the playground, so Maddie bit Lucy and then had to go
to the principal's office. Sawyer's mind begins to drift to Ethan. She
wonders if he'll be wearing the blue polo shirt that accentuates his eyes.

She wonders if she should sit in the front row this time. She wonders if he is thinking about her at that very moment.

"I *said*, what do you think, Mommy?" Matthew says, snapping her out of her thoughts.

"What? Um, I think that's great, honey," she replies.

"*Great*? You think it's great that Maddie bit Lucy?!"

"Honey, is everything OK?" Paul asks, reaching across the table to take Sawyer's hand.

Sawyer glances over at her husband and fears the guilt is written all over her face. "Yeah, everything's fine. Why would you think it isn't?" she asks.

"Well, you're sitting at this table right now, but you're not really here," he says. "And you've just seemed really out of it lately."

"I'm not out of it," Sawyer snaps. "I'm taking two graduate classes and doing consulting work 10 hours a week and parenting a kindergartner. I'm just tired, OK?"

Paul looks stricken. Matthew sticks out his bottom lip, and his face looks exactly the same as Ethan's that evening at Greta's when she announced she was leaving. The guilt is too much for Sawyer.

"I'm so sorry, guys," she says. She looks at Matthew. "Honey, Mommy is just tired. I didn't mean to not pay attention to you." Then she looks at Paul. "I'm sorry, sweetheart. I guess I'm just a little overwhelmed with everything."

Paul's eyes soften, and Sawyer feels a pang of love for him. "It's OK, honey. Just make sure you don't overdo it, OK?"

"I won't," she says, sliding her chair back. "Listen, I think I'm gonna head over to campus a little early, maybe stop in the coffee shop before class. You boys OK here?"

"We're fine," Paul says. "Go get yourself a coffee; get settled. We'll be here when you get home."

He's such a good man, Sawyer thinks, *and I am so unworthy of him.*

She gives him a kiss on the lip, scoops Matthew into her arms for a hug and hurries to the front door. She can't go on like this much longer, she thinks as she grabs her purse and keys. She's going to lose her mind.

Chapter 29

SAWYER GETS TO CAMPUS 35 MINUTES BEFORE CLASS starts and actually does head into the coffee shop. "A medium caramel latte, please," she tells the barista.

"Caramel latte—interesting. That's my daily order," says a voice behind her.

Sawyer's pulse immediately quickens, and she whips around to find Ethan standing mere inches from her. "Ethan! Hi!" she says, flustered.

"Make that two, please," he tells the barista, stepping up and handing over his credit card.

"You don't need to buy my coffee," Sawyer says.

"It's OK—you can get mine next time," Ethan replies.

Next time, Sawyer thinks.

They sidle over to the end of the counter to wait for their drinks. Though they're silent, the energy between them is palpable. When the coffee arrives, Ethan asks Sawyer if she wants to sit down for 15 minutes. "Better than standing around outside my classroom, no?" he asks.

They settle at a table in the corner and Sawyer thinks, *here we go again*.

Ethan takes a sip of his coffee and closes his eyes with pleasure—just like he did after they'd made love and cuddled in his bed. Sawyer fiddles with the cardboard sleeve on her coffee cup. Finally, he breaks the silence.

"How was your weekend?" he asks.

"It was fine," she replies. "Ran errands. Had dinner at my parents' house. Watched Matthew's soccer game. This is his first season!"

Ethan smiles and gets a faraway look in his eyes. "Oh man—soccer! I started playing when I was 5 too. Played all the way through high school. I really loved it. So many great memories!"

Sawyer's ears perk up. "You did? I didn't know that."

"Well, you only gave me one night," he replies.

She feels her cheeks turn pink. "Well, uh … Matthew loves it so far," she says.

"That's awesome," Ethan says, reaching into his pocket and pulling out his cell phone. He scrolls through it and suddenly stops, his face breaking into a wide smile again.

"What?" Sawyer asks.

"Look at this!" he replies and hands her the phone.

Sawyer takes one look at it and gasps. She's looking at the spitting image of Matthew. It's a photo of Ethan as a little boy, kneeling on one knee and resting a soccer ball on the other. He's wearing a red soccer jersey—the same color as Matthew's—and grinning. It's the same crooked smile as Matthew's, the same blue eyes, the same floppy hair.

She must be staring a bit too long, because suddenly Ethan says with a chuckle, "What? Was I that ugly?"

"No!" Sawyer replies. "Quite the opposite, actually. You were adorable. Absolutely adorable."

"Too bad I *was* adorable," he says playfully. When Sawyer continues to stare at the phone, and he realizes she's not going to flirt back, he says, "I'm sure Matthew is adorable in his uniform too. And I *know* you've got a picture on your phone. Let me see one!"

She looks up at him. *This is it,* Sawyer thinks. *This is when he'll put the pieces together and realize Matthew is his.*

She reaches down and takes her phone out of her tote bag. She doesn't have to scroll back very far to find the photo she'd downloaded just four days prior. The soccer league had hired a professional photographer to take photos of the kids before their second game. The photographer had them each pose with the soccer ball on their knee, just like Ethan did in his picture. And of course, since Matthew was their only child, Sawyer and Paul had sprung for the photo package that included a digital file, which she'd downloaded immediately and posted on Facebook.

Sawyer stares at the photo a moment longer before handing Ethan her phone. She watches him as he looks at it, seeing the familiar flicker of recognition in his eyes. *When he asks,* she thinks to herself, *I'm not going to deny it.*

But he doesn't ask. In fact, he doesn't seem to notice the resemblance between him and Matthew. "Oh, gosh!" he says. "Classic soccer pose and same color jersey. What are the odds! He's an extremely cute kid, Sawyer." And he hands her back the phone.

Sawyer quickly shoves it back into her tote. *I should tell him anyway,* she thinks. *I should have him pull his phone back out and show him the two photos side by side.*

But then he says, "Man, it would be fun to have a kid who played soccer. Kick the ball around, teach him some techniques, maybe even coach the team. Too bad I'm never having kids."

Sawyer's head snaps up. "What? You're never having kids?" she asks.

"I mean, I don't plan to," Ethan replies. "It's not that I don't like kids. Kids are awesome. I just can't really see myself having one of my own. I've gotten too used to being alone—too used to just being able to do my own thing. Ya know?"

Sawyer feels tears spring to her eyes, and she suddenly has the desperate need to get out of there. She hastily attempts to pull her sweater on, getting her hands stuck in the sleeves.

"I'm gonna start heading over to class," she says, standing up.

Ethan stands as well. "You sure? We still have another five minutes or so before we need to start walking over."

"Yeah, I'm sure. I just need to make a phone call on the way."

"Are you OK?" he asks. "Did I say something wrong?"

She looks him in the eyes. "I'm fine," she replies. "I'll see you in class."

He throws his hands up and sighs. "OK, then," he tells her. "See you in class."

Sawyer hurries out the door into the crisp fall air, wondering if she should ever tell Ethan—the man who can't see himself having a child—that he actually already has one.

Chapter 30

THE REST OF OCTOBER AND EARLY NOVEMBER SAIL along in a flurry of chaos for Sawyer. She becomes overwhelmed with grad school, volunteering at Matthew's school, soccer and all the Halloween activities and events she never knew existed before she became a mom. She decides to pause her consulting work for the time being, which doesn't seem to alleviate her stress. But the good thing about being so busy is that it gives her less time to obsess over Ethan.

Yes, her heart flutters every Monday evening when she sees him in class. Yes, she feels a jolt of excitement every time his name pops up in her email inbox. But his emails are always schoolwork related, and he no longer tries to pull her aside to chat after class.

Sawyer's relationship with Paul remains comfortable and dependable. They work side by side in the evenings, they take Matthew to all his activities, they tell each other about their respective projects. They sometimes try to watch a movie or show together on weekend evenings after Matthew's asleep, but without fail, one or both of them do not make it through the first half before dozing off.

They have sex only one time that month. It's on a Wednesday evening, after Paul has gone to bed and Sawyer has decided to stay up a bit longer to finish some reading for school. She reads a paragraph that reminds her of something Ethan had said in class, and the thought of his voice, coupled with the glass of Merlot she drank that evening, suddenly floods her with desire. She hurries upstairs to the bedroom, rouses Paul from sleep and jumps on top of him. It's the best sex they've had in a long time, but the thrill of it quickly wears off, because Sawyer lies awake for two hours afterward feeling guilty she'd been thinking of Ethan the whole time.

Sawyer also manages to keep up her weekly brunch/lunch dates with Ava, though now she brings the food over to Ava and Mike's house and basically holds baby Ben the whole time while Ava showers, shoves food down her throat and complains how exhausted she is. Ava does ask about Ethan every time, and Sawyer always changes the subject.

By mid-November, Sawyer begins to feel anxious about school ending soon. The semester will end only eight days after Thanksgiving, and then the Christmas craziness will begin. Sawyer is nervous about her finals. She's nervous about getting all her holiday shopping done, all her cards sent out, all her decorating finished. But if she's being truly honest with herself, her biggest worry is no longer seeing Ethan every week and no longer having an excuse to email him. As much as she has tried to deny it, she loves having Ethan in her life. The thought of losing him completely is terrifying.

And then there's the nagging dilemma of whether she should tell Ethan about Matthew. She hasn't allowed herself to give it much thought, and the more time that passes, the harder she knows it will be if she actually decides to tell him. He will be so, so angry at her for keeping it from him for this long.

All these worries must be written on Sawyer's face when she shows up to class that Monday, because as she makes her way past Ethan's desk, he raises his eyebrows quizzically.

"Can I see you for a moment after class?" he asks her in a low voice. She nods and makes her way to an open seat.

When class ends and the other students begin to file out, Sawyer busies herself with shuffling through some papers, checking her cell phone, rooting through her tote bag in search of an imaginary item. She remains in her seat even after the last student has left and then looks up at Ethan, who leans against his desk with his arms crossed. He gives her a smile so genuine her heart begins to soar. She smiles back, feeling drawn to him but unable to move at the same time.

"You wanted to see me?" she finally asks.

"I did," he replies, his blue eyes boring into hers.

"Well ... here I am," she says. "What's up?"

"Two things," he replies. "First, what's wrong?"

"What do you mean?"

"You didn't seem like yourself earlier when you got to class. I just wanted to make sure everything is OK."

Shit, Sawyer thinks. *He sees right through me.*

"Everything's fine," she tells him. "It's just, you know ... final projects coming up, the holidays. I'm just a little stressed."

"Well, that's the second thing I wanted to talk to you about," Ethan says. "Everyone is stressed this time of year—especially grad students. So, I'm hosting a relaxation workshop at the studio on Saturday. There will be some yoga, some meditation, a little aromatherapy. It's full, but I always leave an extra spot open at these special events in case anyone I know wants to come. And, um ... I'd love for you to come, Sawyer. It'll give you a chance to see the studio, and to see me outside of professor mode."

YES! Sawyer thinks, but she stays quiet.

"I'm assuming Matthew's soccer season is over …" Ethan continues.

She nods. "Yes, last Saturday was the last game."

"Good," Ethan says. "So come. It's 10 a.m. until noon, and I think you'll really enjoy it."

Sawyer's mind is racing. It's telling her to say no. *No, I've got too many errands to run. No, I've got to study for finals. No, I should take Matthew to the playground.*

But Sawyer knows those are only excuses. In fact, Paul has plans to take Matthew to a kids workshop at Home Depot to build wooden Christmas ornaments on Saturday morning, and Sawyer was probably just going to hop on the treadmill and do laundry. If it weren't Ethan who'd invited her, Sawyer would normally jump at the chance to go to a free yoga workshop. But the fact of the matter was, it *was* Ethan who'd invited her. And Sawyer knows she'd be going to the workshop as much to see him as she would to do yoga.

"Fine—suit yourself," Ethan says, turning to put his stuff into his briefcase.

"No, no—I'll go!" Sawyer tells him. "I'd love to see the studio. And you're right—I could definitely use some destressing."

There's that dazzling smile again. "Great!" he tells her. "Try to be there by 9:45. I'll save you the best spot—right up front."

"You'd better!" says Sawyer, and she finally gets up from her seat.

That night, she has a dream that she and Ethan are making love on a yoga mat in an ashram in India. She startles awake and sees Paul sleeping soundly beside her. *My God*, she thinks to herself. *What am I doing?*

Chapter 31

"SO, WAIT—YOU SAID IT'S YOUR *PROFESSOR* WHO'S running this workshop?" Paul asks Saturday morning as they're having breakfast.

Sawyer has the audacity to feel annoyed with Paul for obviously not listening when she told him about the workshop earlier that week. "Yes, I *told* you. He owns the studio and teaches a couple of classes on the side."

Paul doesn't sense her annoyance. "That's weird—a grad school professor teaching yoga," he says.

Sawyer feels strangely defensive. "Why is that weird?"

Paul just chuckles. "Sorry—it's not weird at all," he says. Then he leans over and extends his fist toward Matthew. "You and I, buddy—we're gonna do *manly* things!"

Matthew fist-bumps Paul. "Yeah, we're gonna *build* things!" he says.

Sawyer slides her chair back in a huff and brings her plate over to the trash can, where she scrapes off the remainder of her pancakes. "Men do yoga, Paul," she says. "Way to teach our son gender stereotypes!"

Paul, still oblivious to just how perturbed his wife is, comes over and puts his arms around Sawyer from behind. "Oh, honey—I'm just teasing!" he says, resting his chin on her shoulder. "Matthew and I are just gonna miss you—aren't we, little man?"

"Yes!" Matthew replies.

And just like that, Sawyer's annoyance is replaced by an even worse feeling—guilt. She turns around and gives Paul a kiss on the lips. "I'm gonna miss you boys, too. But go, have fun, do your manly things. And then this evening we'll have movie night."

"Yay!" Matthew shouts.

"All right, honey. Go get Zen," Paul says.

Somehow, Sawyer believes this workshop will be anything but Zen for her.

She drives the 20 minutes to Harrison and finds a spot in the parking garage Ethan had recommended via text the day before. She then uses her cell phone GPS to walk the four minutes to Ethan's studio, which sits on a street corner at the edge of downtown Harrison.

She glances at the time. 9:24. Darn. It's *way* too early to go in there now. She looks around to see if there's a coffee shop or something she can pop into when the studio door opens. Out steps Ethan, wearing lightweight black joggers, a loose blue sleeveless tee, a black headband pushing his blond waves back and black Adidas slides. His face lights up.

"Sawyer! Hi!" he says. "I was just running up to my apartment to grab my water bottle. Why don't you go on in, and I'll be right down?"

Sawyer can't help but notice his biceps, and she shivers both from the cold and the spasm of desire that shoots through her. "OK," she says.

He holds the door open for her, and she steps inside. "Be right back," he says again, and the door closes behind him.

Sawyer turns and gasps in awe as she takes in her surroundings. The studio is just the way she envisioned it from Ethan's description, but even better. The front and right walls are glass garage doors with aqua rolldown shades, while the back wall is exposed brick. The left wall, painted a soft gray, is lined with benches topped with plush aqua pillows. Cubbies underneath allow yogis to store their shoes and coats. Dim lighting falls on lots of floor plants, and an eight-foot chalkboard easel in the back corner says "Namaste" in big aqua letters. A warm, cozy feeling washes over Sawyer.

The door opens behind her and Ethan steps inside. "What do you think?" he asks earnestly.

Sawyer turns and looks him in the eyes. "It's amazing, Ethan. Absolutely amazing."

He smiles proudly, and she can't help noticing the pink that spreads across his cheeks. "You have no idea how much that means to me, Sawyer," he says.

A force field fills the space between them as they stand there, transfixed. Sawyer can't seem to look away from those blue eyes. She's turning over words in her head, trying to figure out what to say, when the door opens behind Ethan and a gorgeous, twentysomething blonde woman breezes into the studio. She's sporting camo-print leggings and a black crop top, and her hair is pulled into a messy bun. She's carrying a rolled-up aqua yoga mat under her arm, as if she purposely bought it to match the studio's cushions. And she looks just as surprised to see Sawyer as Sawyer is to see her.

"Oh, wow!" she says. "Someone actually beat me here today!"

Ethan turns around and does a little bow. "Good morning, Ashley. We have a newcomer joining us today. Her name is Sawyer."

Ashley very obviously looks Sawyer up and down and gives her a half-smile. "Sawyer," she repeats. "I know a few Sawyers, but they're all guys."

Sawyer fights the overwhelming urge to reach up and yank on Ashley's bun. Instead, she smiles back coolly. "Yeah, well ... some of us are too unique to have a common name."

Ethan quickly steps between the two women, trying to hide his amusement. "Sawyer, Ashley was one of my first clients."

"And obviously your best client," Ashley replies, giggling. Sawyer rolls her eyes as Ashley steps into the room and unrolls her yoga mat in the spot directly in front of Ethan 's mat.

"Actually, Ashley, I was going to have Sawyer be front and center today. She's brand new to yoga and will need some extra attention," Ethan says.

"No, really, Ethan—I'd be better off in the back," Sawyer says quickly. "I have no idea what I'm doing."

"Yeah—you don't want everyone to watch her and do the wrong thing," Ashley sneers.

"Everyone who signed up for the workshop is a regular," Ethan replies. "They all know what they're doing and won't be looking at anyone else for guidance."

Ashley glares at Ethan, glances over at Sawyer and looks back at Ethan. When she realizes he's not going to budge, she sighs loudly and slides her mat over. Sawyer would have laughed out loud if she weren't feeling so nervous about being front and center.

Ethan turns back to Sawyer and winks, and she feels her heart race. "OK, Sawyer, I've got a mat for you in the back. Let's get you all set up, and everyone else should start arriving in the next 10 minutes or so, OK?"

"OK," Sawyer replies. "Let's do this."

Chapter 32

TWO HOURS LATER, AS THE WORKSHOP IS COMING to an end, Sawyer feels like she's floating. All the self-doubt, stress and anxiety she felt when she arrived at the studio has been replaced by a sense of calm and well-being. For the first time in as long as she can remember, she's not ruminating about something that happened in the past, or fretting about something she needs to do or worrying about the future. She's just *being*. She's living in the moment, soaking in the lingering scent of the aromatherapy and the sounds of the soft music Ethan has playing. A feeling of strength has taken over her body.

"Thank you for joining us this morning," Ethan says after leading the class through one last series of deep breaths. "Let's continue to be mindful the rest of the day and take our good thoughts and peace with us. Namaste."

"Namaste," the women (and one man) surrounding Sawyer murmur.

Everyone gets up and begins to shuffle about, spraying down and rolling up their mats, putting on coats and shoes, chatting about their plans for the rest of the day. Several of the women tell Sawyer it was nice to meet her and that she did great, or they ask if they'll be seeing her at the studio again. They all give off such a supportive, familial vibe … all except Ashley, who's now sitting on a bench and taking an extra-long time to lace up her sneakers.

Soon, every student except Sawyer and Ashley has left. Sawyer is standing awkwardly by Ethan's desk, and Ashley is still sitting on the bench. It's officially a standoff at the yoga studio.

Ethan finishes inputting a few things into the computer and shuts it down. As he comes around the desk, Ashley stands up. Ethan regards her in a calm and friendly manner, as if he's been through this rodeo before.

"Wonderful job today as always, Ashley. I'll see you in Hatha Yoga on Tuesday."

She beams. "Thank you, Ethan. I think I finally perfected my Hanumanasana."

"Yes, yes—I noticed," he replies.

There's an awkward silence, and Sawyer is beginning to wonder if she should leave when Ethan asks, "Is there anything else I can help you with today, Ashley?"

The younger woman, who annoyingly looks even hotter now that her bun is messier, looks over at Sawyer, then back at Ethan. "Yes, um … I was wondering if we could work on what you've been teaching me."

Ethan gives Sawyer a quick glance, just long enough for her to notice it. *What exactly is going on here?* Sawyer wonders.

"Ashley, you know your private lesson isn't until Thursday with Andrea," he replies. "I only filled in for her this past week because her daughter was sick. Just keep practicing, and she'll be ready to work with you on Thursday."

Ashley brazenly walks over to Ethan and plants her entire body inches in front of him. Sawyer half expects her to peel off her yoga pants right then and there and throw herself at him. She's struck by how jealous she feels, and at the same time, by how overwhelmingly attractive Ethan appears as she watches this beautiful twentysomething throw herself at him.

"I'd rather learn from the best," Ashley says. "And what else do you have to do, anyway? Do you have a hot date or something?"

Sawyer's eyebrows shoot up, but Ethan doesn't miss a beat. "As a matter of fact, I do, Ashley."

This is clearly not the answer Ashley was expecting to hear. She takes a jerky step back as if Ethan has just slapped her. Her armor is cracking right before Sawyer's eyes. "Oh…" she says, looking over at Sawyer as if his date can't possibly be her. "Oh … OK. I guess I'll see you on Tuesday, then."

Ethan nods. "Yes, Tuesday. Now if you'll excuse me, I'm just gonna go over membership options with Sawyer here. Drive safely."

Even Sawyer can feel the sting Ashley must be feeling, and she'd almost feel sorry for her if she weren't such a wretched woman. "Yeah … I will," Ashley replies coolly. She picks up her mat and water bottle and walks out, letting the door slam noisily behind her.

Ethan turns to Sawyer. "O-*kay* then," he says. "How about some lunch?"

Sawyer feels bold and inspired by what she just witnessed. Ashley is too young to have learned the art of subtle flirting, but Sawyer is not. "Lunch?" she replies. "What about your hot date?"

Ethan gives her that glorious smile. "I'm looking at her," he replies.

Sawyer's heart is pounding so strongly, she is convinced Ethan can hear it. Paul flashes into her mind, and she knows she shouldn't play along. But she also knows that she's never felt more alive in her entire life than she does at this moment. She has to do whatever she can to keep that feeling from disappearing.

"If you mean hot temperature-wise, then you'd be correct," she tells him. "I'm sweaty and sticky, and I'm wearing yoga clothes. So, unless you're taking me to lunch at McDonald's, I'd say I'm not prepared for the occasion."

"Oh, I had a different place in mind," he says.

"Oh, yeah? Where?"

He steps closer to her, nearly as close as Ashley had been to him a few minutes earlier. "It's a place with impeccable service," he says.

Sawyer swallows hard. "What's it called?" she asks softly.

"Chez Porter," he replies. "Only the finest ingredients." He tilts his head up toward the ceiling and his apartment.

And suddenly, Sawyer knows this is one of those pivotal moments in her life—a moment in which everything can change based on the decision she makes. She feels like she's in the middle of a tug-of-war game, one side pulling her toward Paul and Matthew and her stable and comfortable life, and the other pulling her toward Ethan and this feeling of exhilaration and inspiration and passion and connection that she's never felt before. And there's another feeling there, a feeling she can't quite figure out, and then she does figure it out, and *holy shit*—it's love. She loves Ethan. She has always loved Ethan, from that first moment she met him in the gazebo at Ava and Mike's wedding. She knows she should feel afraid of that love, but in that moment, Sawyer doesn't feel afraid. She feels safe.

"OK," she says. "Take me upstairs to Chez Porter."

He bows. "At your service." She follows him out the door, as he locks up the yoga studio. She shivers both from the crisp air and the anticipation of what's to come.

Chapter 33

ETHAN'S APARTMENT IS AN EXTENSION OF THE YOGA studio. It has the same industrial feel times ten—exposed brick, dark wood floors, a black metal spiral staircase leading to an open-loft bedroom and a bathroom. The first level is all one open space. The kitchen has dark wood cabinets and granite countertops. There's a breakfast bar with aqua-cushioned stools, which is where Ethan clearly eats his meals, because in the adjacent dining area there's a pool table where a dining table should be. Opposite the kitchen is the living space, which has a giant flat-screen TV on the wall and an oversize gray sectional with deep cushions. Next to the living space is a makeshift workout corner, with a punching bag hanging from the ceiling, a set of weights, a Peloton and a rolled-up yoga mat. There are also bookshelves lined with books, potted floor plants in every corner and lots of windows with the same aqua rolldown shades as in the studio. It's a grown-up version of a bachelor pad, quite the opposite of Sawyer's house, and yet so cozy and homey.

"Wow," Sawyer says as she takes it all in. "Ethan—this place is *amazing!*"

"Thank you," Ethan says proudly. "I worked really hard on it, and I have to admit, I love it too. And the best part is, I don't have to worry about disturbing the downstairs neighbors except when there are classes going on," he says, stomping his feet on the wooden floors.

Sawyer chuckles. "Yeah, no raucous parties during business hours."

"Because I have *so* many friends to invite to parties," Ethan replies sarcastically, rolling his eyes.

Sawyer had never thought about how strange it is that Ethan is such a loner when he's such an incredible person. But she supposes that's part of what attracts her so much to him—the fact that he trusts her enough to let her in when he's spent his whole life building walls. It's not that he's not a nice guy—he's one of the friendliest people she knows, and everyone is drawn to him. It's just that he doesn't let people get too close to him. And now here he is, inviting her into his personal space.

Ethan takes her coat and shoes and puts them into the coat closet. He points to the spiral staircase. "The bathroom is up those stairs and to the right if you need it," he tells her.

"Yes, I'll just go wash up," Sawyer replies.

When she gets upstairs, she finds the bathroom to be quite luxurious for such a manly apartment. There's a large, old-fashioned white clawfoot tub that's also a shower, gray railroad-tiled floors and a white vanity with a raised rectangular sink. The walls are the same aqua Ethan used throughout the studio and the rest of the apartment.

Sawyer washes up and carefully heads back down the stairs, wondering how Ethan navigates them after a night of drinking. Then she realizes yoga studio-owning professors probably don't overindulge on alcohol very often. She finds Ethan in the kitchen, washing some salad greens in the sink with a gray dish towel draped over his shoulder.

"All set?" he asks her.

"Yes!" Sawyer replies. "Man, what I wouldn't give for a warm bath in that tub of yours."

"Go ahead and take one!" Ethan says. "I can get lunch done while you do that."

Sawyer feels herself flush. "That sounds lovely, but the last thing I would want to do is put these sweaty clothes back on."

"Throw them in the washing machine, and I can give you a T-shirt and drawstring sweats to wear while they dry," he tells her.

A jolt of pleasure runs through Sawyer as she remembers wearing Ethan's T-shirt and sweats to bed on the one night they spent together, followed by a stab of guilt as she thinks about the fact that the shirt is currently hidden in a bin in her attic, mixed in with her old concert and college T-shirts. She'd never been able to bring herself to get rid of it, even after she and Paul got married and moved into their current house. She wonders for a minute if her bridesmaid dress from Ava's wedding is hidden somewhere in this apartment, and then she chastises herself for what a ridiculous thought that is. Ethan probably got rid of the dress as soon as he realized she had disappeared on him.

"Sawyer? Everything OK?" he asks her.

"Yes," Sawyer says, snapping out of her trance. "I'm good. Let me help you make lunch."

Ethan shrugs. "If you say so! But the offer still stands to use the bathtub if you change your mind."

They work side-by-side in the kitchen with a comfort and ease that shouldn't surprise Sawyer, but they do. Sawyer chops veggies for the salad while Ethan grills turkey, gruyere and avocado sandwiches on multigrain bread on his panini press. Then he mixes up his "famous salad dressing" while Sawyer cracks open two cans of High Noon and pours them into glasses. When they're finished, they sit side-by-side at the breakfast bar, clink their glasses and sip.

"Cheers to your first yoga class," Ethan says. "What did you think?"

"Oh my God, I *loved* it!" Sawyer replies. I felt so … centered afterward."

"I told you you'd love it," Ethan says. "You should come to more classes! I'll give you the friends and family discount—unlimited classes for zero dollars a month."

Sawyer smiles as she swallows a mouthful of salad. "Please," she says. "I can't accept favors from my professor."

"Is that all I am to you?" Ethan asks. "Your professor?"

"Of course not," Sawyer replies. "But I definitely shouldn't be accepting a free yoga membership from you. And even this, what we're doing right now … it's inappropriate."

"What, having lunch?" Ethan asks.

"Ethan—come on," Sawyer says. "We are having lunch and alcoholic beverages together *in your apartment*. It's definitely unethical. What if someone thought our friendship was influencing my grade?"

Ethan touches Sawyer's hand. It's a friendly gesture, but it drives her wild all the same. "Well, I guess I'll just have to fail you so no one gets the wrong idea," he jokes.

She punches his arm, and he chuckles and shakes his head. "No—all kidding aside, Sawyer, your work speaks for itself. There's no way that anyone can question your good grades. Plus, the semester will be over in a couple weeks, and then … then I won't be your professor anymore."

They eat their sandwiches—which are delicious, by the way—in silence for a few minutes as they both ponder what the end of the semester will mean for them. Sawyer wonders if Ethan is just as nervous as she is about not seeing each other in class every week. She knows that joining the yoga studio is a way for her to stay in his life, and she wonders how often she could feasibly drive there for classes. Twice a week, at most.

"Does your silence mean you're considering it?" Ethan asks.

Sawyer nods. "I'm considering it."

He smiles. "Good."

They finish their lunch, and Sawyer helps Ethan wash the dishes and glasses and put everything away. She glances at the microwave to check the time. It's 1:37. Shoot. Paul and Matthew are expecting her home already. She wonders if Paul tried to call her, but she doesn't want to check her cell phone, which is on silent in her coat pocket in Ethan's closet.

Ethan must have seen her look at the clock because he suddenly turns sad. "Do you have to go now?" he asks softly.

Sawyer looks at the time again. 1:38. "Oh man, Ethan. I don't want to go. I *should*, though."

He takes a step closer to her. "One more drink," he says. "Let's just talk a little more and then you can go."

"I can't drink more," Sawyer replies. "I have to drive home, and I'm a lightweight."

Ethan laughs. "I remember," he says, prompting her to lightly shove him in the stomach and feel his rock-hard abs. "I'm kidding … sort of!"

Chapter 34

BUT IT WORKS, BECAUSE A FEW MINUTES LATER Sawyer finds herself next to Ethan on the sectional, taking a sip of his High Noon, which this time he is drinking straight from the can. She hands the can back to him and sinks back into the oversize cushion. "Oh, man—this is *heaven*!" she declares. "Where did you get it?"

"Arhaus," he replies. "I paid an arm and a leg for it, but it was worth every penny."

"Yes, indeed!" Sawyer says, closing her eyes. She feels Ethan sink back into the cushion next to her; she feels the heat between their bodies. When she looks over at him, he's already staring at her. They stay that way for what seems like hours.

"What?" he says.

"*What?*" she replies.

"What are you thinking about?"

She sighs, wondering how honest she should be. Should she tell him she is marveling over the powerful resemblance between him and Matthew? No. She can't ruin this moment. So instead, she asks in her most playful voice, "What is *up* with that girl Ashley?"

Ethan laughs out loud. "I was starting to wonder what was taking you so long to ask about her!"

"Oh, my *gosh*!" Sawyer continues. "I thought she was going to strip down and try to have sex with you right there!"

"Don't think she hasn't tried," Ethan says. And there it is again—that stab of jealousy like a dagger through Sawyer's heart. She looks back up at the ceiling.

"Like I said earlier, Ashley was one of my first yoga students, so she's been coming to the studio almost a year now. She's been … interested from the beginning."

"You've been fighting her off for almost a *year*?" Sawyer asks incredulously.

Ethan chuckles. "I wouldn't say I've been *fighting* her off. She's pretty harmless."

"I wouldn't be so sure about that. She's pretty relentless—and gorgeous."

"Do I sense a hint of jealousy?" Ethan asks.

"Why would I be jealous?" Sawyer asks a little too quickly, her face burning up. She focuses on a tiny dark smudge on the ceiling, a small blemish on Ethan's otherwise perfect apartment. "I just think it's funny."

"I don't think it's funny at all," Ethan says. "I actually feel sorry for her."

"I don't. I think she needs to learn how to take a hint."

"Well, not everyone is as good at taking a hint as I was six years ago."

And there it is. Tears spring into Sawyer's eyes. The ceiling smudge starts to blur as she fights to hold them in. Ethan must still be looking at her, must see the tears forming, because he says her name ever so softly. Then she feels his hand on her chin as he turns her face toward his. He is inches away, and she sees that he, too, is fighting back tears. She tries to look away again, but she can't.

"Ethan ..." she says as a single tear escapes her left eye and starts to roll down her cheek. "Ethan, I'm ... I'm sorry. I'm so sorry I disappeared on you."

He wipes away the rogue tear with his thumb. "It's OK, Sawyer. I understand. I'm just so happy I found you again."

Sawyer knows she should turn away; she should grab her stuff from the coat closet and go home to Paul and Matthew. But she can't move. She is stuck on that couch next to Ethan like a plant whose roots have grown into the cushion.

"I want to kiss you right now," Ethan whispers, his hand still cradling her chin. "But if I do, there is no taking it back ..."

He wants her consent—she knows that—but she can't give it. She can't say yes or even nod her head, but she can't say no either. She continues to stare at him, transfixed, as if she is allowing him to see into her soul. And then, ever so slowly, he leans forward, and when she doesn't pull away, Ethan gently places his lips on hers.

It's a feeling more powerful than anything Sawyer has felt before. It's as if she can feel the Earth shift back into equilibrium, as if she's been lost for an eternity and is finally home. Yes, Paul and Matthew are her home, but this—this is a different kind of home.

They hold their lips together for a few amazing moments. Then Ethan shifts forward on the sofa, turns his body toward Sawyer, and takes her face in both his hands. She feels him gently nudge her lips apart with his own, and she doesn't resist. She feels his tongue inside her mouth, searching for hers, and then she finally gives in. She grabs his face and kisses him back hungrily, every cell in her body alive with pleasure. She falls back onto the couch and he moves on top of her, running his lips along her face, her ears, her neck. She feels worshipped; she feels adored; she feels loved. It is only when she feels Ethan's hand on her belly, underneath her shirt, that Sawyer pulls away. He pulls back and gazes at her with such love in his eyes that she begins to cry, and he sinks down on the couch next to her and wraps her in his arms.

"Sssshhh …" he whispers into her ear. "It's OK, Sawyer. It's all going to be OK. I love you."

"I love you, too," she whispers back. And they remain like that for another 30 minutes, clinging to each other as if their very lives depend on it. It is Ethan who finally breaks the silence.

"Sawyer," he says softly. "I think you'd better go now."

"I don't want to go."

"I don't want you to, either. But I also don't want you to get in trouble."

She sighs. She's not ready to face the world, to deal with this new reality and all that comes with it. She wants to stay here forever in this cocoon, with this man she loves so much. But Ethan is right. She has to go.

Sawyer sits up, and Ethan does too. He gazes at her with those eyes—so much love in those blue eyes. "What are we going to do?" she asks meekly.

He lets out a long breath. "I don't know, Sawyer. This … this is uncharted territory."

She nods. "I know. I—I can't believe I'm doing this. I'm not a bad person, Ethan, I swear."

"Sshh sshh sshh," he says, pushing a rogue piece of hair behind her ear. "I know you're not a bad person, Sawyer. You're a wonderful person. The best kind of person. But you're human. And this … this is something that goes beyond any reason. And it's something that's impossible to ignore."

He's right about that last part—Sawyer knows that. But she is *married*, to an incredible man who'd do anything for her. And Ethan is

Matthew's father, and Sawyer has kept that from him. He trusts her, but she is lying to him. And how can she tell him now? He'd be crushed. He thinks she's a good person, but she's not. She's lying to him, she's lying to Paul ... she is a terrible, awful person. Sawyer starts to cry again.

"Sawyer, please ... talk to me. Let me help you," Ethan says.

Sawyer shakes her head. "You can't Ethan," she says. "You said it yourself. There's no taking it back."

Ethan looks stricken. "Do you want to take it back?"

"Yes!" Sawyer wails. "No. I mean—I don't know, Ethan. All I know is this isn't me. I'm not a person who cheats on her husband."

"But you're not happy ..."

"I'm not *un*happy," she replies. "I have a beautiful life, Ethan. A beautiful home, an amazing kid, a great husband. I just feel like something is missing. I feel unfulfilled."

He takes her hand. "Don't you feel like maybe it was me that was missing?"

She buries her head in her hands. Ethan is right—he is exactly what was missing from her life. The kiss confirmed that. For so long she's been craving the kind of connection she has with Ethan. And she loves him, plain and simple, beyond reason. But she also loves Paul and their life together. And she made a commitment to him. He was there for her when no one else was. He was there for her *son* when he needed a father. And she can't just throw that all away.

"Ethan ..." she says. "I wouldn't take it back. I wouldn't. But it can't happen again, OK? I can't sneak around with you and still be the kind of person I want to be. I can't. I don't want to live a lie."

He closes his eyes and throws his head back like she has driven a dagger through his heart. Then he pinches the bridge of his nose between his fingers. "I understand, Sawyer. It's just ..."

"It's just what?"

"Don't you feel like you're already living a lie?"

It's as if she's been slapped in the face. It's true, what he's just said, but it doesn't make it any less painful. And she's angry at him for putting it out there. She can't take it. She stands up and dashes over to the coat closet to get her stuff.

"Sawyer, wait," he says. "Look at me."

"No," she tells him as she hurriedly pulls on her coat. "I have to go now, Ethan. I'll see you in class on Monday."

"Sawyer, please!" he calls after her as she opens his front door and hurries down the stairs. "I can't lose you again! I understand if we can only be friends. Just please don't disappear on me. Please."

She stops at the bottom of the staircase and turns to look up at him. "I won't disappear, Ethan. I promise."

And she turns around again and walks out the door into the cool air.

Chapter 35

SAWYER BURSTS INTO TEARS AGAIN AS SHE TURNS into her long driveway a short time later. A flood of guilt and shame washes over her. She'd seen the colorful sidewalk-chalk creations at the end of the driveway behind Paul's BMW, some of which had clearly not been drawn by a 5-year-old. *Paul is such a good dad*, she thinks. *Why can't that be enough for me?*

She takes a few deep breaths before getting out of the car and walking to the front door. She realizes her heart is pounding. When she got in the car after leaving Ethan's house, she looked at her phone and saw she had a missed call and two texts from Paul.

So much fun at Home Depot! Headed to Red Robin for lunch, the first one read.

Then, 90 minutes later: **Heading home now. Where are you? M wants to wait for you to watch a movie.**

She'd written back that she was on her way home, and he hadn't responded. He is going to be *so* angry with her. Sawyer goes over various excuses in her mind for her lateness. *She stayed for another class. She decided to run some errands. There was an accident on the highway.* But when Sawyer gets inside, she finds Paul in the three-car garage—what he calls his "man cave"—organizing some boxes.

"Hey, you!" he says happily. "How was your class?"

Relief washes through Sawyer, followed by exasperation. She realizes that Paul doesn't even notice, or care, what time it is and that she should have been home hours ago. Part of that—a *big* part of that—is that he trusts her, and that part makes her happy. But she *wants* him to notice how late she is. She *wants* him to worry about where she was and what she was doing. She *wants* him to *pay attention*!

"Where's Matthew?" she asks.

"Jackson's house," he replies. "They were driving by while we were doing sidewalk chalk, and Jackson rolled down the window and asked if Matthew could come play. You weren't home yet, so I said it was OK."

You weren't home yet. Sawyer goes over the words in her mind, trying to detect a hint of curiosity, or accusation, or *something* in his voice, but there's nothing there. He's simply stating a fact.

"Well, I guess I'll go up and shower and then walk over and get him," Sawyer says.

"OK, babe. I'm just gonna go through a few more of these boxes and then I'll be inside," Paul replies, barely looking up.

She waits. She knows she shouldn't test him, but she can't help herself. "I'm taking a shower … in a kid-less house. I can take a nice, long, steamy one."

She wants him to raise his eyebrows and say something suggestive. She wants him to stop what he's doing and follow her upstairs into the shower. She wants him to look at her like he can't go another minute without ravaging her body—the way Ethan looks at her. But all he says is, "You deserve it!"

Sawyer's heart sinks, and she turns and lets the door slam shut behind her. The guilt and shame she felt only minutes before is replaced by disappointment, annoyance and emptiness. As she showers, letting the hot water pour over her body, she remembers Ava's words to her—that this lack of passion is normal in a marriage. And maybe Ava's right—maybe it *is* normal. But she doesn't want normal. She wants to feel with Paul the way she feels with Ethan. But can she—especially now that she has found Ethan again? She doesn't know, but she sure as hell wants to try.

Chapter 36

THE REST OF SAWYER'S AFTERNOON AND EVENING IS
a portrait of domestic suburban life. She goes over to the Brauns' house
after her shower to pick up Matthew and ends up staying for coffee
with Angie. When she and Matthew get home, Paul orders an early
dinner from a local Chinese restaurant—Matthew loves the lo mein—
and they eat it picnic-style on a sheet spread out on the family room
floor. Matthew insists on watching *The Polar Express*, even though Paul
has a general rule that they don't start Christmas in their house until after Thanksgiving. But with Turkey Day only five days away and
Matthew showing his adorable boo-boo lip, Paul gives in.

When the movie is over, Paul gives Matthew his bath while Sawyer
cleans up the remnants of their feast. Sawyer reads Matthew a book—
The Polar Express, which it had taken her a good 10 minutes to find
and dig out of the dusty bin labeled "holiday books" in the storage
room—then gives him a snuggle before Paul arrives to take her place.
This is their nightly routine—Sawyer reads and cuddles with Matthew,
then Paul comes in and lies down with him until he falls asleep. It's
something Paul started when Matthew was 2 and transitioned from

his crib to his toddler bed. In those first couple weeks, Matthew would come out of his room incessantly and beg for "cuddle time." Sawyer was of the school of thought that children should learn to fall asleep on their own. She would go inside, lie down with him a few minutes, then give him a kiss and leave. Two minutes later, out he'd come asking for "more cuddle time." It was Paul, with his tender heart, who would always give in and climb into bed with Matthew until he drifted off to sleep, which usually took between 10 and 15 minutes. Matthew got so used to it that soon, all he wanted when he went to bed was Paul. He couldn't fall asleep without Paul. It bothered Sawyer that the very thing she wanted to avoid had happened, but she figured it was Paul's thing, and since he didn't mind, she let it go.

But over the past year, the nighttime ritual had started to bother Sawyer more and more. Matthew started taking longer to fall asleep, and between Paul's demanding job and the rigors of parenting, he often fell asleep in Matthew's bed as well. In the beginning, Sawyer would sneak in and wake him up so they could spend time together, but that usually made Paul disoriented and cranky. So gradually, she started getting into other things while Paul was sleeping in Matthew's bed—work, a TV show that Paul hated like *This Is Us*, a gossipy phone call with Ava—and by the time he crawled into their bed, she was already asleep.

It was a horrible rut to have fallen into, but Sawyer had always pushed it out of her mind and written it off as just another casualty of being parents. But now that Ethan is back in her life, she realizes just how much it bothers her and how much it has damaged her relationship with Paul. Still, she isn't sure how they can break the cycle at this point. She too is exhausted and preoccupied in the evenings now, and she doesn't have the energy or the patience to train Matthew to fall asleep on his own again. It is easier to just continue the way things are.

On this night, though, Paul insists that he won't fall asleep and that he'll come to bed as soon as Matthew's asleep. He tells Sawyer to wait for him. So, she changes out of her flannel pajamas and cotton briefs and into the black silky underwear and matching bra that she bought for her first date with Paul. She lights a candle on her nightstand and climbs into bed, scrolling through Facebook on her phone to avoid falling asleep. And she waits. And waits.

The next morning, Sawyer wakes up under the covers, still wearing the black bra and underwear. She rolls over to find Paul asleep on his side with his back to her. The candle is out. She doesn't remember blowing it out the night before and wonders if Paul did. She also doesn't remember whether Paul had tried to wake her up when he came to bed, or if he had even noticed that she was wearing her "special occasion" bra and underwear.

Sawyer picks her phone up off the nightstand and glances at it. 6:47 a.m. She sighs and throws the covers off, picking up her ball of pajamas from the floor and pulling them on. She tiptoes out of the bedroom and pads down the hallway to the stairs. Matthew's door is still closed, which means that, mercifully, he's still asleep. She heads down to the kitchen and brews herself a K-Cup of hazelnut coffee with the Keurig. She pulls a vanilla yogurt and some strawberries out of the fridge, and she is just sitting down at the kitchen table when her phone screen lights up. It's a text from Ethan.

Not sure if you're awake. Couldn't sleep. Can we talk?

Sawyer closes her eyes and takes a deep breath as the anxiety floods back in. She is happy—so, so happy—to hear from Ethan. But she doesn't *want* to be happy to hear from him. She wants to be the woman who tells him to please leave her alone, that she's happily married. But she can't. She just can't.

Not today, she writes instead. **I need some time to think. Can we talk after class tomorrow?**

Absolutely, he replies. **I'm sorry for what happened, Sawyer. But I'm not sorry for the way I feel.**

She starts to cry. She wants to write back to Ethan, but every time she starts to type something, it doesn't feel quite right and she ends up deleting it. So instead, she texts Ava.

You up?

Her phone rings almost immediately. Sawyer snatches it up and hurries down to the basement and into the exercise room, where she shuts the door. "That was quick!" she says.

"You're texting me at 7:15 on a Sunday morning," Ava replies. "Something has to be up. Talk to me, Seesaw."

"Where's Nate?" Sawyer asks.

"Still sleeping. And so is Mike," Ava replies. "Now spill it. What happened?"

Sawyer tells Ava the whole story, from the yoga workshop to the kiss on his couch to the "I love yous" that came after. To her credit, Ava remains quiet, listening intently. When Sawyer is finally finished, all she hears is silence.

"You still there?" Sawyer asks.

She hears a loud sigh on the other end. "I'm just … trying to gather my thoughts here, Sawyer," Ava says.

Sawyer cringes. Whenever Ava calls her by her real name, it means she's upset with her. Sawyer had thought it would feel good to confide in Ava and get everything off her chest, but now she's worried that she should have kept her mouth shut.

"Do you hate me?" Sawyer asks.

"Of course, I don't hate you," Ava replies. "I'm just … disappointed."

Sawyer feels like a kid who got caught eating contraband candy, or a teenager who got caught sneaking out of the house. She hates to disappoint people, especially Ava.

"I'm disappointed in myself," she replies. "But I have a really big problem here, Ava. I love Ethan."

"But what about Paul, Sawyer? Don't you love him?"

"Of course, I love him! I do. But it's a different kind of love."

"It's *real* love, Sawyer. What you have with Ethan is infatuation. It's new. You know it wouldn't be that way forever, and if you're not careful, you're going to throw away something real, something good."

"It's *not* new," Sawyer says. "It's been six years, Ava. *Six*. And it hasn't gone away. You know I never stopped thinking about him."

"That's because you never got closure. And now he is here again and all you're thinking about is this one magical night you had with him. That's not real life, Sawyer. What you have with Paul—*that's* real life."

Sawyer thinks about this. "I don't know, Ava. I can't help wondering if Ethan is the one I was supposed to be with all this time."

Now Ava sounds angry. "Sawyer, are you *crazy?*" she asks. "If you were supposed to be with him, you would have been. But you left him after that night for a reason. He disappeared for a reason. It's because it wasn't meant to be. Please, Sawyer. Please don't throw away this beautiful life, this beautiful family, that you have for a man you actually don't know all that well. You feel like you're in love now, Sawyer, but you don't know if things with him are sustainable."

"You're right, Ava. I'm not going to walk away from Paul. But I won't cut Ethan out of my life. I can't."

"You *have* to, Sawyer! You have two weeks left of school. How are you going to keep seeing him when he's not your professor anymore?"

"I was thinking I could join his yoga studio …"

"And keep lying to Paul? Keep telling him Ethan's just your yoga teacher and not the father of your baby?"

Sawyer stays quiet. Her head hurts. Finally, Ava speaks again. "Look, Sawyer—I know this is hard. But it's not too late to get yourself back on track. What happened is done. You can't change it. You can only control what you do moving forward. And you can't keep seeing Ethan and lying to Paul."

"So, what are you saying? I should tell Paul I kissed Ethan? Tell him I love Ethan? Tell them both that Ethan is Matthew's biological father?"

Ava sighs as she gathers her thoughts. "Look, I am all about honesty. You know that. And I was the one who urged you from the beginning to be honest with both of them. But things have changed now. And this is one of those situations in which the truth would do no good. It would only hurt Paul, it would hurt Ethan, it would hurt *Matthew*. And Ethan told you himself he doesn't want kids."

"That's true …"

"This is not the lifestyle Ethan wants, Sawyer. He's a free spirit. He doesn't want to be a father and live in the suburbs. Paul does. And he loves you. So you need to finish out the semester, and then you and Ethan need to go your separate ways. Do whatever you need to do to get the closure you need and move on. I know you may think you love him, but you have a family that needs you. So forget about the kiss, and just move forward."

She quiets down and gives Sawyer the space to cry her tears and feel her feels. Sawyer knows Ava is right. But how is she supposed to just forget about such a powerful experience? How is she supposed to move forward and act like such a life-altering moment never happened?

"I have to tell Paul," Sawyer finally says.

"Tell Paul what?" Ava asks. "That you kissed another man? That you have *feelings* for another man?"

"Yes."

"Sawyer … listen to me. Do *not* tell Paul. Please."

"Why not? Because you think he'll leave me? You think he'll throw me out of the house?"

"I don't, actually," Ava says. "I don't think Paul would ever leave you and Matthew. I think Paul is in it for the long haul, through thick and thin. But I do think this would crush him, Sawyer. It would absolutely devastate him. And for what? For you to clear your conscience?"

Suddenly, Ethan's words pop into Sawyer's head, and she says them aloud.

"Because if I don't tell him, I'll be living a lie."

"Your life is not a lie, Sawyer. The love you have for Paul and Matthew is real. The life you have built together is real. This thing with Ethan … it's just a teeny tiny part of you. It's not all of you. And all the *good* parts of you that Paul knows and loves are real. We all lose our way sometimes, and that's all this is. You lost your way. But I know my best friend, and I know you can find your way back from this."

"Thanks, Ava," Sawyer says, wiping away her tears. "I love you so much."

"I love you too, Seesaw. Truly. But I hear Nate on the monitor, so I have to go. Just take a deep breath and try to calm down. Go have a nice day with your family. And we will take this one day at a time."

Chapter 37

THE FOLLOWING EVENING, SAWYER WALKS INTO THE building where her class is held with her stomach tied up in knots. She is feeling so many emotions at once. The thought of seeing Ethan gives her butterflies. She feels exhilarated. But mixed in with that anticipation and excitement is nausea and fear. She wants to run from him as badly as she wants to run *to* him.

She's 20 minutes early and had planned to go right to class, but she heads to the lobby lounge instead to try to gather herself. She doesn't want Ethan to see what a bundle of nerves she is. She feels like she is going to have a panic attack and starts doing some deep breathing until several other students peek over at her with curiosity. She gets up, walks to the elevator and back again, then back to the elevator, and finally she gets on. When she gets to her classroom, she steadies herself, then walks in and heads straight to a seat in the back without looking up. She's aware of a buzz around her; her classmates are talking more than they usually do only five minutes before class starts. She bends over to pull her laptop out of her tote bag when Myra, the girl sitting to her left, says, "Have you talked to Ethan at all?"

Sawyer freezes. Has word somehow gotten out already about their kiss? "No, I haven't. Why?"

Myra jerks her head toward the front of the room. "He's not here. No one knows why. He hasn't canceled class or anything."

Sawyer looks up. Sure enough, Ethan's desk is empty. She feels a panic start to rise up in her throat. She hadn't heard from Ethan at all after their text exchange the previous morning. He hadn't said anything to her about not coming to class today. He wouldn't ditch his entire class just to avoid her, would he? No, he wouldn't. Something must be wrong.

Sawyer swallows and looks at Myra, trying not to reveal her emotions. "Um, that's weird. Has anyone tried to email him?"

"A bunch of us have," Dave, the scruffy hipster guy sitting in front of them, replies.

Andrea, the Zoe Saldana lookalike sitting to his right, turns and says smugly, "I just tried calling his cell phone twice. He didn't answer."

Sawyer pushes down the pang of jealousy she feels at this knowledge that her beautiful young classmate has Ethan's cell phone number. *He probably gave it to her for a school-related reason*, she thinks. *Which is not what's important right now! What is wrong with me?*

For the next 20 minutes, the students continue to discuss what might be going on. Sawyer feels more and more frantic with each passing minute. She pulls out her cell phone and taps out text after text.

Where are you? We are all here in class.

Are you OK? Did something happen?

Please answer. I'm getting worried.

Finally, a guy in the front row stands up and begins to gather his stuff. "Well, he's obviously not coming," he says. "I say we all just go home and report this to the front office in the morning."

The other students stand up and start to gather their belongings as well. Some of them seem relieved to be going home early on this Monday evening three days before Thanksgiving. Sawyer remains in her seat and stares at Ethan's empty desk, her brain working a mile a minute.

"Sawyer, you coming?" Myra asks. "There's no sense in sitting here all evening."

"I, um … yeah, I'm coming," Sawyer replies. She slides her laptop back into her bag, stands up and files out of the classroom behind Myra and the last of her classmates.

"You wanna head to the library and study for the final with me?" Myra asks.

But Sawyer knows there's no way she can study. And she can't go home, either.

Suddenly, she knows what she has to do.

"Um, I think I'm just gonna go home," she tells Myra. "I'm pretty tired.

"OK," Myra says. "Have a great Thanksgiving!"

Sawyer hightails it to the parking lot and practically dives into her car. She plugs Ethan's address into her GPS and begins to speed, willing the cops not to pull her over. The closer she gets to the studio and apartment, the harder her chest pounds. She feels a strange sense of foreboding. The last time she went searching for Ethan at home, he was gone.

As she exits the highway and enters Ethan's neighborhood, Sawyer's ears begin to buzz. She prays it's not a migraine coming on. A migraine is the last thing she needs right now. But no, it's not a migraine. It's the sound of a siren in the distance. She exhales with relief.

Sawyer drives a few more blocks and hears another siren. She pictures an elderly woman or man being taken from a home on a stretcher and says a quick prayer. She hopes the paramedics arrived in time.

She turns onto the main road of Downtown Harrison and finds herself stuck in a line of cars. She's only eight blocks away from Ethan's place. What is *up* with all this traffic? It's crawling ahead at a snail's pace, and Sawyer is getting more and more frantic. She is desperate to get to Ethan. Seven blocks away. Six. Five. Suddenly, Sawyer sees lights everywhere. At first, she can't register where they are coming from, but then she spots police cars along the side of the road. What is happening?

Four blocks away. Sawyer sees ambulances. Three blocks away. Groups of people huddled on the sidewalks. Two blocks. Fire trucks. And then, when she's only a block away from Ethan's place, Sawyer gasps. She sees smoky air. She sees chaos. And she sees the remnants of Ethan's apartment and yoga studio, burned down to nothing more than a charred shell, looking every bit the picture of dashed dreams.

Chapter 38

THE TRAFFIC IS DIVERTED TO THE SIDE STREETS, and Sawyer turns right. But instead of continuing to follow the other vehicles, she pulls over in front of a parked police car. She jumps out of her SUV and begins to hurry down the sidewalk. A young police officer approaches her.

"Ma'am, you can't leave your car here. This is a crime scene, and we need to keep space open for more officers and detectives."

"A crime scene? There was a fire!"

"We have reason to believe it was arson, ma'am. We're investigating it."

Sawyer begins to shake. "Did … did anyone …?"

"There were no casualties, ma'am. Now, please move your car."

Sawyer feels relief, followed by a fresh wave of panic. "Please, officer—my friend lives there. My *good* friend. I just want to make sure he's all right."

"I'm sorry, ma'am. Why don't you just give him a call?"

"Please!" Sawyer shouts, feeling herself lose control. "He's not answering his phone. His whole life was in that building. Please."

The officer sighs and shakes his head. He looks around dramatical-ly, as if he's about to tell her a really juicy secret. And then he leans in conspiratorially and whispers, "OK, fine—go. But don't leave your car here too long."

Sawyer takes off down the sidewalk. She gets to the corner across from Ethan's apartment and strains her eyes to get a better view. Police officers and firefighters are milling about in front of the charred studio, trying to determine what happened.

Sawyer looks around frantically. A group of people are gathered on the sidewalk across the street, just behind the police tape. Sawyer hur-ries across the street, past the officer who's diverting traffic. She joins the group, trying to figure out if Ethan is among them.

"It's such a shame," one woman says. "He just opened that studio barely a year ago."

"They're saying it's arson. Who would do such a thing?" asks another.

"Excuse me," Sawyer says. "I'm looking for Ethan—the owner. Has anyone seen him?"

The first woman tilts her head back toward the side street behind her and lowers her voice. "He's sitting alone back there," she says. "He's pretty shaken up."

Sawyer doesn't even take the time to thank her; she jogs down the sidewalk until she finds Ethan sitting on the curb between two parked cars, his head in his hands. She steps up behind him. "Ethan …"

He startles and looks up at her with tearful eyes. "Sawyer … oh, my God, Sawyer." He buries his face in his hands again.

Sawyer sits down in the small space between him and a silver Toyota Camry. "Ethan, I am so, so sorry."

She feels his body settle into hers. "Who would do this, Sawyer?" he asks. "My studio. My apartment. I lost everything."

"I don't know, Ethan," she says, rubbing his back. "But you haven't lost everything. You have me. And you're safe."

He pulls away from her and wipes his face with his hands. Then he shakes his head. "I worked so hard on that place. I finally achieved my dream. I finally had a place that felt like home to me. And it's all gone."

"Well, what did they say?" Sawyer asks. "What happens now?"

"They said insurance will cover it and I can rebuild," he tells her. "Like that's supposed to make me feel better. I'm starting from scratch now. I can't even wrap my brain around what will need to be done."

"OK, well, we'll take it one step at a time," Sawyer says. "For now, though, maybe you should start by calling your mom."

Ethan stiffens. "Sawyer, you know that's not gonna happen."

"But maybe this will be an opportunity for you two to reconnect …"

"I said *no*, Sawyer. I'm not gonna suddenly call my mom when I need something from her."

Sawyer is about to protest again, but she stops herself. Ethan had told her a bit about his mother and their relationship on the first night they spent together, but he made it clear this was a topic he wasn't willing to discuss any further. All Sawyer knew was that Ethan's mother had left him and his father when he was only 7 years old. She'd fallen in love with a neighbor who'd recently gotten divorced and moved to another city with him. They'd since had two more children, but Ethan had only met them one time seven years ago, when they'd shown up at his father's funeral with his mother. Ethan had coolly introduced himself and then demanded that they leave immediately and never contact him again. He had no interest in forming a relationship with them or in reconciling with his mother.

Sawyer starts to think about how different Ethan's family situation is from Paul's—how lucky Matthew is to have two sets of grandparents that dote on him and an aunt, uncle and cousin who are such big parts of his life. She wonders how Ethan's mother would feel if she knew she had such an amazing grandson—how his half siblings would react if they knew they had a nephew. Then she shakes her head and brings herself back to the current moment. Right now, all that matters is being there for Ethan. She realizes he's still talking.

"So they said I can stay at the Residence Inn just down the street for a few months while the renovations are being done, and then put in for reimbursement …"

"Ethan, stop," Sawyer interrupts. "Don't be ridiculous. You're coming and staying with us."

He looks at her and shakes his head. "Are you out of your mind, Sawyer? I'm not coming and crashing with you and your *husband!* And your *kid!*"

"Yes, you are," Sawyer says. "You can stay in the pool house. It's fully furnished, it has heat and a full kitchen, and it's way more comfortable than a Residence Inn."

He lets out a chuckle that is far from good-natured. "Yeah, of course you have a pool house."

Sawyer feels her cheeks burn with shame. "Yes, I have a pool house that I never use," she says. "And I can't think of a better way to use it."

"Absolutely not," Ethan says. "It's not happening."

But then she reaches over and grabs his hand and she feels him softening. She is so confused; she has no idea what to do about this whole messed up situation with Ethan, but right now she'll say anything to get him to agree to come with her.

"Ethan … I want you to come," she tells him. "Please. We only have two more classes before the semester ends and without the yoga studio, I'll have no reason to see you after that. I know things are complicated, and I know it's going to be awkward, but I'd really feel a lot better if you were nearby. Please … if you love me like you say you do, let me help you."

He lets out a long, loud breath and looks over at her. She stares back at him, willing herself not to look away, and feels as if she can see into his soul. She can see all the pain in his eyes, but also all the love he has for her.

"Fine," he finally says. "I'll stay with you. But what do we do about Paul?"

"What do you mean?" she asks.

"I mean, what are you going to tell him about me? Do you know how fucked up it is to have me come live in his house if he doesn't know who I am or anything that's happened between us?"

"Of course I do, Ethan. But what choice do we have right now?"

The question hangs in the air for a while. Finally, Ethan stands up. "OK … I've got to go talk to the police, find out next steps and everything. I can't get down the next street where the garage is, so I'll have to ride with you. Is that OK?"

"Of course it's OK!"

"Thanks. Where are you parked?"

She tells him and stands up as well. "I'll wait for you in the car."

He nods and walks off past the whispering onlookers while Sawyer walks to her car, wondering how Paul is going to react to their new houseguest.

Chapter 39

THEY PULL INTO SAWYER'S DRIVEWAY AN HOUR LAT-
er after a fairly silent ride. Ethan hadn't been in the mood to do much
talking, and Sawyer was too nervous about what she would say to Paul
when they got home. Ethan takes a long look at the house and shakes
his head. "I guess now I'll get a taste of how the other half lives," he
says.

Sawyer puts the car in park and glares at him. "Ethan, I get it,
OK? I'm rich and I have a disgustingly big house and I don't deserve it.
There, are you happy now?"

His face softens. "Of course, you deserve it, Sawyer. Forgive me. It's
just that I've lost everything ..."

A tear escapes his eye and slides down his cheek, and Sawyer has
the overwhelming urge to reach over and take him into her arms. But
the lights are still on in the house; Paul could walk out to greet her at
any moment.

"Come on, let's go," she tells him.

Ethan shakes his head. "I'll wait here. You go inside first and tell
Paul the situation. It's better that way."

She thinks about it for a minute and realizes Ethan is right. "OK, she says. "I'll leave the car running so the heat stays on. I'll be right back."

He nods, and she gets out of the car and hurries up the front walk. Sawyer punches a code into the keypad to unlock her front door and sprints into the foyer. She places her bag on the floor but leaves her coat and shoes on. "Hello?" she calls out.

"In here!" she hears from Paul's office.

She makes her way to the office and finds him sitting at his desk, typing something on the computer. He lights up when he sees her, and she fights off a pang of guilt. "Hey there!" he says. "I was wondering when you'd be home. Did you stay late to study again?"

"Paul … I need to talk to you," she says.

He looks back at the computer screen and begins to type again. "What is it, babe?"

She pulls out the large leather chair on the other side of the desk and sits down. "Paul, this is important," she says.

He keeps typing. "OK, give me a second … I just need to shoot off this email."

"*Paul!* I'm serious!"

He stops typing and stiffens when he sees her expression.

"What is it, babe?"

"Remember when I told you about Ethan, my professor?"

"Yeah … the yoga guy," he says.

Sawyer nearly rolls her eyes but stops herself. "Well … he didn't show up to class tonight," she says. "We all waited 30 minutes and then left. And I decided to go over to his apartment to see if he was OK."

A suspicious expression immediately crosses Paul's face. "How do you know where he lives?"

"Because I went to his yoga workshop, remember? He lives on top of the studio."

"OK … well why would you go over there? Maybe he's sick or something."

"He's not sick. When I got there, I drove into a crime scene, Paul. His apartment and the yoga studio were burned down. They think it was arson."

Paul's expression changes. "Holy *shit*, Sawyer. Was he inside?"

"He was at home, getting ready to leave for class. He had his keys in his hand and everything. He smelled the smoke right away and was able to get out of there quickly."

"Thank God," Paul says.

"Yeah … but he lost everything. Insurance is going to cover the renovations, but he'll have nowhere to live for a few months."

"Can't he stay with family?"

"He doesn't have any family."

"Can't they put him up in a hotel or something?"

"They can … but it's a whole process for him to get reimbursed. Plus, it's the holidays, Paul. I'd hate to think of this guy alone in a hotel room for the holidays."

"So what are you saying, Sawyer?"

"I'm saying that I think we should let him stay in the pool house."

Paul's eyebrows shoot up. "The pool house," he repeats.

She nods. "We're always saying what a shame it is that it doesn't get more use, Paul. So why not help him out and let him stay there?"

"Because he's your *professor*, Sawyer. That's freakin' weird."

"He's my professor for two more classes," Sawyer says.

"This is crazy! What about his friends? He doesn't have any friends who can take him in?"

"No one with the extra space that we have, Paul," Sawyer says. "There's no reason for us not to help this guy out."

Paul sighs and loudly closes his laptop. "I don't know, Sawyer. It's not just us living here. We have a kid. What about Matthew?"

"What *about* Matthew?" Sawyer asks, thinking about the night her boy was conceived and immediately hating herself for it.

"You don't know this guy from Adam, Sawyer. You've had a few classes with him. You went to one yoga workshop. What if he's, like, a criminal or something?"

Sawyer feels herself getting angry and wills herself to keep her cool. "Paul. He's been background checked by the university. He's not a serial killer. He's just a good person who needs help, and we are fortunate enough to have the means to give it. If we're not going to help people when they're in need, what's the purpose of having all of this?"

Paul leans forward and rests his elbows on the desk, rubbing his temples with his fingers. Then he sighs. "OK, Sawyer, fine. If this is that important to you, go ahead and call him and tell him he can stay in the pool house."

Sawyer practically starts jumping up and down. "Oh, Paul—thank you *so* much! Really, you have no idea how much this means to me. I'll go get him."

Paul stands up. "Wait a minute—go get him? What do you mean, 'go get him?' "

"Oh … he's in the driveway. In the car."

"Wait, what? You drove him here? *Without asking me?*" Paul shouts.

"Sssshhhh—you're going to wake up Matthew!"

"How could you bring him here without even calling me?" Paul asks in a slightly lower voice. "So you were just going through the motions when you asked me if he could stay here, weren't you? You were going to let him stay here whether I said yes or not!"

"Paul—that's not true. That's the reason he's still in the car. If you said no, I would have driven him to a hotel."

Paul starts pacing back and forth. "You backed me into a corner here, Sawyer. If I had said no, and then you told me the guy was already *in my driveway*, I would have looked like a total jerk. I would have *had* to change my mind and say yes. It's not fair how you went about this, Sawyer."

Sawyer doesn't respond. What can she say? Paul is right. Finally, he stops pacing and sighs. "Whatever, Sawyer. It is what it is. The guy is here now, and I'm not gonna turn him away. Go out and get him."

A surge of love rises to her chest, and Sawyer steps forward to hug her husband. "Thank you, Paul. Thank you for being so understanding. The guy lost everything. I couldn't just leave him there in front of his burned-down home and studio."

"I know, Sawyer. Just go and get him."

Chapter 40

SAWYER'S HEART RACES AS SHE STEPS THROUGH THE front door with Ethan behind her. Bringing him into her home is surreal, but she doesn't want to let herself think about it too much or the guilt will consume her. Paul steps into the foyer, trying to appear casual.

"Honey, this is Ethan," Sawyer says shakily.

Ethan finishes removing his shoes and steps out from behind Sawyer with his hand outstretched. "It is so nice to meet you, Paul. Thank you so much for letting me crash here for a bit."

Paul hesitates a moment, then shakes Ethan's hand. "No problem. I'm sorry to hear what happened."

The two men stare at each other for an excruciating length of time as Sawyer looks back and forth at them. Ethan has a look of confused interest on his face as he takes in the tall, dark, handsome, clean-cut Paul, who is so different from his own scruffy, laid-back vibe. But it's Paul's expression that makes Sawyer truly uncomfortable. He's looking at Ethan the way someone would if they spotted a celebrity on the street and couldn't remember what movie or TV show the person had starred in. It's an I-know-you-from-somewhere look of recognition.

For a minute, Sawyer wonders if perhaps Paul *does* know Ethan from somewhere—a thought that's scary in and of itself. But then she realizes the more likely scenario—that Paul sees the striking resemblance between Ethan and Matthew, that perhaps he's putting the pieces together in his mind. So she quickly moves next to Paul and slips her arm around his waist. She sees the hurt flash quickly across Ethan's face, but she figures that's better than allowing Paul's internal analysis to continue. And besides, if Ethan is going to stay in their pool house, he's going to have to get used to seeing her and Paul together.

"Ethan, why don't I grab you a bottle of water from the fridge and something to eat if you're hungry? Then Paul and I can show you to the pool house, and you can get settled. After I bring Matthew to the bus stop tomorrow morning, I can drive you back to get your car out of the garage, and you can go do some shopping to get whatever you need."

Ethan locks eyes with Sawyer and holds her gaze, clearly perturbed by the detached tone of her voice. "Water would be great, but I'm not hungry, so no need for any food. Thank you."

"OK ..." Sawyer says. "I'll go grab you a bottle."

"That's OK, Sawyer," Paul interjects. "I'll get Ethan some water and show him out to the pool house. You go on upstairs and get ready for bed. I'm sure you're tired after such a long evening."

"No, no, you go finish your work. I'll show Ethan out."

"I *said* I've got him," Paul says sternly. And he fixes Sawyer with a look that tells her not to argue.

"Um ... OK. I'll see you upstairs, then. Good night, Ethan."

"Good night, Sawyer."

She turns and heads up the stairs on shaky legs, wanting nothing more than to bring Ethan out to the pool house herself and assure him that everything will be OK. But the truth is, she doesn't know if that's the case.

Chapter 41

THE NEXT MORNING, SAWYER IS STARTLED OUT OF A deep sleep by a hand touching her cheek. She opens her eyes to find Matthew standing there, achingly adorable in his fleece Pokémon pajamas and his crazy bedhead. "Good morning, Mommy," he says.

Sawyer's heart melts, and she reaches out to envelop him in a tight hug. "Good morning, sweetheart. What time is it?"

She picks up her cell phone from the nightstand and turns it on. "6:03 a.m.! No wonder my alarm hadn't gone off yet! Why are you up so early?"

Matthew shrugs. "I don't know. Guess my body was just ready to wake up."

Sawyer giggles. She loves what she and Paul refer to as their son's "Matthew-isms." He is constantly surprising them with the words that come out of his mouth.

"Guess so!" she replies. "Too bad mine isn't."

Sawyer usually sets her alarm for 6:32 on weekday mornings—6:32 exactly, not 6:30. (For some reason, those extra two minutes feel like two hours.) She takes 30 minutes or so to drink her coffee and eat a small breakfast at the kitchen island while she glances through *The New York Times*. Then she wakes Matthew up a little after 7 to do his morning routine. He has to be at the bus stop by 8:05 a.m.

On these rare mornings that Matthew decides to wake up earlier, it always throws her off balance, and she feels like the day starts off on shaky ground. But then Sawyer remembers that Ethan is in her pool house at this very moment, and she realizes that today—and every day moving forward—will feel off balance.

"Come *on*, Mommy! Let's go downstairs!" Matthew insists.

"OK, OK—I'm coming, little man," Sawyer says. She slowly rises out of bed and pulls on her fluffy white robe. She and Paul had spent a long weekend at a spa resort in Scottsdale, Arizona a couple years back, and Sawyer had fallen so in love with the spa robes there that he'd bought her one. She loves the robe and always pulls it on over her pajamas on chilly mornings.

"Oh, boy—Mommy needs coffee!" she says, sliding her feet into her Ugg slippers. She takes Matthew's hand, and they pad down the stairs and into the kitchen, where she finds a note from Paul on the island.

Went in early to make sure everything gets done before my leave starts. Hopefully won't be too late. Xoxo, Paul.

Sawyer sighs. Today is the last day of school before Thanksgiving break starts for Matthew, and Sawyer had convinced Paul to take tomorrow—the day before Thanksgiving—off so they could do something as a family, since her class was cancelled. They had decided to spend the day in New York City doing touristy things with Matthew, then head over to see the Macy's Thanksgiving Day Parade balloons being inflated. Sawyer had been so excited, but now she just feels strange about having this perfect family day while Ethan is all alone in the pool house.

Sawyer brews herself a hazelnut K-Cup, then serves Matthew his favorite breakfast—cinnamon Eggo waffles, apple slices and a cup of milk. She lets him play a game on his iPad while he eats so she can read the paper a bit. Just as she's about to take Matthew upstairs to get him dressed, there's a tap on the sliding glass door that leads to the back deck. She looks up and gasps when she sees Ethan standing there, wearing Paul's favorite Yankees hoodie and a pair of blue Adidas sweatpants that appear to be Paul's as well.

Sawyer jumps up and rushes over to the door to let Ethan in. She hadn't been expecting him to come into the house this morning and isn't prepared to introduce him to Matthew yet, but she's not about to leave him shivering out there in the cold.

"Ethan! is everything OK?" she asks.

"Yeah, everything's fine, and I'm sorry to bother you. It's just that I didn't grab my phone charger when I was leaving the apartment yesterday and now my battery is dead, and I really need to have my phone available in case the detectives or the insurance company call."

"Oh, yes, of course! I can grab you an extra charger!"

Sawyer turns around and nearly bumps into Matthew, who is standing behind her and gazing curiously up at this stranger who's just turned up in his kitchen. *This is it*, Sawyer thinks.

She takes a big swallow and a deep breath and says, "Matthew, this is Mommy's friend, Ethan. He's going to be staying in our pool house for a few months. Ethan, this is Matthew … my son."

Sawyer fears that Matthew will feel shy or awkward, but he just steps forward and waves up at Ethan with friendly blue eyes. "Hi, Mr. Ethan!"

Ethan smiles down at him and takes his hand to shake it. "Hey there, buddy! You can just call me Ethan."

Sawyer searches for any glimmer of recognition in Ethan's eyes, but there is none. She can't believe it. Seeing the two of them together is surreal for her. To her, the resemblance is so strong that anyone who sees the them together would know they are father and son. But that seems lost on Ethan.

"OK. Then hi, *Ethan*," Matthew says proudly.

Ethan laughs. "I love your pajamas, buddy. Who is your favorite Pokémon?"

Matthew's face lights up. "Pikachu, of course!"

"Of course," Ethan says. "But you know which one Pokémon I love most? Charizard!"

"*You* like Pokémon too?" Matthew asks.

"Do I like Pokémon?" Ethan repeats in an incredulous voice. "Come on, now? Who doesn't like Pokémon?"

"My daddy."

Oh, my God—AWKWARD! Sawyer thinks. But Ethan doesn't skip a beat. "Well, I'm sure he likes other cool things, buddy."

"Not really," Matthew says matter-of-factly.

Sawyer hastily steps forward. "OK, Matthew. It's time to get you ready for school, or you're going to miss the bus."

"Wanna see my Pokémon cards after school?" Matthew asks Ethan.

"Honey, I'm sure Ethan is going to be very busy …"

"Nonsense!" Ethan says. "I'd love to see your cards, little man."

"Yay!" Matthew says. "Come on, Mommy! I want to wear my Pikachu shirt today."

Sawyer looks at Ethan. "Thank you. Let me get you that charger, and then I'll get ready to drive you to your car when I get back from the bus stop."

"No rush. It's not like I have anywhere else to go!"

Sawyer laughs with admiration. She is astonished by Ethan's optimism and positivity even in the face of tragedy. She hopes it's a trait that was genetically passed on to Matthew.

Chapter 42

SAWYER MANAGES TO GET MATTHEW READY QUICKLY and take him to the bus stop with two minutes to spare. She hurries back home to shower and get dressed and spends a little more time on her makeup than she normally would. Then she heads out to the pool house and knocks gently on the door. Ethan opens it instantly, as if he'd been waiting for her.

"Would you like to come inside my humble abode?" he asks.

She giggles. "That's very kind of you, sir. But I believe we should hit the road."

"Very well, then," he says. "Let me just get my shoes on."

He closes the door and reappears a minute later with the key in his hand. As he locks up, Sawyer sees him shiver.

"Is it warm enough in there?" she asks. They begin to walk around the house toward Sawyer's car.

"Absolutely," he replies. "Just a bit nippy out here."

"I can run back in the house and get you one of Paul's coats," Sawyer offers.

He shakes his head. "Nah, that's OK. I'll be heading to the mall after I get my car to buy some things. I already feel weird borrowing his hoodie and sweatpants."

They make it to the driveway, where Sawyer's SUV—which she'd already pre-started from inside the house—is waiting, warm and toasty. They climb inside.

"How did that come about, anyway?" Sawyer asks. "Did he offer his clothes to you?"

"He did, when he was getting ready to show me to the pool house. He grabbed them from the clean laundry pile in the laundry room. It was very nice of him."

Sawyer glances at Ethan and tries to read his facial expression, but it's blank. She backs out of the driveway and pulls onto the road.

"So … what did you two talk about?" she asks.

"Not much, really. Just some small talk."

"That's it?"

"That's it."

"Did he seem … cool about everything?"

"As cool as any guy would be while showing a strange man into his pool house."

"Fair enough," Sawyer says.

They're quiet for the rest of the ride, the awkwardness of their current situation hanging in the air between them. As they near Ethan's apartment and studio, she asks if she should take him there or straight to the garage down the block to get his car.

"The garage," he replies. "The fire department is meeting me here at 1 to escort me inside and see if there's anything I can salvage. I figure I can get some errands done before then."

"OK … do you want me to stick around and help you? As long as I leave by 3 to get Matthew from the bus …"

"No, it's OK, Sawyer. You've done so much for me. Thank you, though."

Sawyer's heart sinks a bit. Just as she pulls into the parking garage, Ethan's cell phone rings. He looks at the screen. "It's the police department," he says.

"Oh—answer it!" Sawyer says.

"Hello? Yes, this is Ethan Porter," he says, followed by a long pause. You're kidding me.

Ethan pauses again.

"She *confessed*? When?"

Sawyer inches a little closer to try and hear the officer on the other end as Ethan listens.

"Yeah, I can come now, actually." Ethan pauses as he listens to the officer. "OK, great. Thank you. I'll be there soon."

He hangs up and stares stone-faced out the windshield.

"What is it, Ethan? Someone confessed to burning down the studio?"

He nods. "Yeah. And you'll never believe who it was."

"*Who?*"

"It was Ashley."

Sawyer has to think for a minute before she realizes who he's talking about. Then her eyes widen. "*Ashley*? Holy shit, Ethan! That girl from the yoga workshop who was all over you?"

He nods. "Yeah. Apparently, she walked into the police station a little while ago and turned herself in."

"What the heck? Why the hell would she *burn down your studio*? I knew that girl seemed crazy, but not *that* crazy!"

He clears his throat. "She, uh … she told the detective who questioned her that she and I had a 'thing.' Which we didn't. And she said that she found out there was another woman and just snapped."

"Another woman? Who?"

He turns to her with sad eyes. "Sawyer, after she left the workshop, she watched the studio from her car. She saw you come up to my apartment. The next day she showed up at class, even though she doesn't usually go on Sundays, and confronted me about it. She asked me flat-out if you and I were seeing each other."

"And what did you say?"

He closes his eyes to steel himself. "I told her we were."

"*Ethan*! What the hell? Why would you tell her that?"

"Because I was tired of constantly having to reject her. And … I felt sorry for her."

"You felt *sorry* for her?"

"I did, Sawyer. I knew her self-esteem was taking a hit. I figured if I told her you and I were seeing each other, she'd see it less as a rejection of *her*. So I told her you were an old flame who'd come back into my life and that I felt like I needed to see where things would go."

Sawyer sighs. She hates the idea of Ethan telling *anyone* that they are seeing each other, considering they had only one kiss and that she is a *married woman*. But she can't help but admire Ethan's tender heart and his attempt to soften the blow for Ashley.

"OK, I get it. And how did she react?"

"She went nuts. Completely freaked out. She started crying and hitting me and telling me I'd been stringing her along. I tried to reason with her, but she wasn't being rational. She finally said she was canceling her membership and wanted nothing more to do with me and she stormed out. I knew she was really upset, Sawyer, but I had no idea she would do *this*."

Sawyer doesn't know what to say. This is the kind of stuff she reads about in books or sees in movies—a scorned woman going crazy and doing something drastic. But she can't imagine someone doing something like that in *real life*. She thinks back to when her past relationships had ended and how angry she'd been. Sure, she'd been tempted to break a car window or two. But *this*? Burning down someone's business? Someone's *home*?

Sawyer shakes her head. "I don't know what to say, Ethan. She did it around 6 p.m., right? It had just gotten dark outside. She was pretty brazen to do it then as opposed to the middle of the night."

"She told the detective that she knows I teach Monday nights and that the studio is closed. She wanted to do it when she knew I wasn't home. She said she wasn't trying to kill me. Unfortunately, I was running a little late yesterday. I don't know how she managed to do it without anyone seeing her. I have to go to the station now to get all the details."

"She didn't want to kill you. Gee, that was kind of her," Sawyer says sarcastically.

"Sawyer, please. The girl is clearly insane."

There he goes again, Sawyer thinks. *Feeling compassion for others even when they destroy his life. This is why he has been so kind to me even though I disappeared on him. I don't deserve his kindness. I'm a piece of shit.*

Her mind continues to race. *Oh my God—it's my fault that Ashley burned down his building! It's because she saw me with him. If I hadn't gone to his apartment, he'd still have a home. Still have a studio. Oh my God, I'm ruining his life!*

Sawyer begins to shake as the panic rises through her chest. "Ethan, I have to go," she says. "Good luck at the station."

"You OK?" he asks.

She nods, but she can't look at him. "I'm fine," she says. "It's just … this is a lot to process."

"It is," he says. "I've got a long day ahead of me. I'll see you later, OK?"

She nods, and as soon as he gets out of the car and closes the door behind him, she peels away, wishing she could just keep driving forever and ever.

Chapter 43

SAWYER DOESN'T SEE ETHAN THAT EVENING. SHE sees the lights go on in the pool house about 9 p.m. while she's studying at the kitchen table and texts to ask if he is OK. He says yes, he had a long day and has another busy day ahead of him tomorrow, so he's going to crash. She wants so badly to walk out to the pool house and knock on the door, but she resists. When she heads up to bed a little while later, Paul makes a move on her for the first time in a long time, and they have sex. She senses a feeling of urgency about it coming from him.

The next day goes exactly as planned. Sawyer, Paul and Matthew head into the city around 11 a.m. They go ice skating at Rockefeller Center, shop at FAO Schwarz and the LEGO store, and watch the Thanksgiving balloons inflate. They eat gooey, dripping pizza slices for lunch and steaming bowls of pasta at an Italian restaurant for dinner.

It's a magical day, and Sawyer frequently reminds herself how lucky she is to be able to provide this kind of life for her son. She does her best to stay in the moment and enjoy everything, but she can't resist the thoughts of Ethan that continue to pop into her head. She wonders what he's doing, whether he's OK, what's going on with Ashley. She feels guilty to be spending this day with her family in the city, while he is all alone after having just lost everything. She feels guilty about thinking of him when she should be fully focused on her family. She even feels guilty at the thought of Ashley being in prison on Thanksgiving because of her decision to go up to Ethan's apartment. It's an enormous amount of shame to deal with, but Sawyer does her best to focus on Matthew and his squeals of delight throughout the day.

When they finally get back into the BMW to head home, Matthew immediately falls asleep in his car seat, and Sawyer leans her head back and sighs.

"We did it," she says. "We survived the crazy holiday crowds and gave our boy the perfect New York City day."

"We did!" Paul says. "And we finally got to do those touristy things that most people from the area never do!"

Sawyer closes her eyes, feeling physically and emotionally drained. They drive in silence for a few moments as Paul toggles through the radio stations before settling on the "80's on 8" station on XM radio. 'Til Tuesday's "Voices Carry" is on, a song Sawyer and Paul always dissolve into laughter over because when it came on the radio when they first started dating, Sawyer sang the words "you're so scary" instead of "voices carry" and insisted to Paul that those were the proper lyrics. When she Googled them and found that she had, in fact, been singing the incorrect lyrics all her life, she laughed until she cried. But today, she says nothing.

"You're so scary!" Paul sings along with the tune. When Sawyer doesn't laugh or respond, he leans over and grabs her hand. "What's wrong? Tired?"

"Very," she says.

More silence. "Sawyer, come on," Paul says. "I know something is bothering you. What is it?"

She takes a deep breath. "It's just … I feel bad that Ethan is going to be alone tomorrow on Thanksgiving. Maybe we should invite him to your parents' house."

She feels Paul's hand tense up.

"I mean … they wouldn't mind, right? They're so welcoming of everyone," Sawyer says.

"No, they wouldn't mind," Paul agrees. "It's just … don't you think it's a little much? He moves into our home and now he's coming to Thanksgiving dinner?"

"He didn't move into our home, Paul," Sawyer says with annoyance. "He's crashing in our pool house because *his apartment burned down.*"

"I'm well aware of that, Sawyer," Paul replies. "I just don't get why the dude would even want to come to Thanksgiving dinner with a bunch of strange people."

"Strange people?" Sawyer asks.

"Yes, Sawyer!" Paul says, his voice rising. He pauses a minute as Matthew rouses from sleep and shifts in his car seat, then falls back asleep. "You've been in, what, 10 classes as his student? And you went to a yoga class. And he literally met me once. I know he's estranged from his family, but if the guy doesn't have any friends he can spend Thanksgiving with instead of one of his *students*, there's something very wrong here, Sawyer."

He's right—she knows that—and Sawyer wonders if she should admit to Paul that she'd known Ethan since before she became his student. She could tell him that she'd kept it quiet because of the potential conflict of interest around being in his class. But no, she can't open that can of worms right now.

"Fine … we'll let the guy spend Thanksgiving alone in the pool house," she says. "How very generous of us."

Paul sighs. "That's just lovely, Sawyer. Make me feel like an asshole."

"I'm just stating the facts."

"Yeah, I'm sure you are," Paul says. "Whatever. Invite the guy to Thanksgiving. Invite whomever you want. I don't care anymore."

"Paul, come on …"

"This is exactly what you did to me on Monday, Sawyer. You asked me if we could let him stay with us when you were going to let him no matter what I said. And now you ask me about inviting him to Thanksgiving when you couldn't care less what my answer is. So maybe you should save yourself the trouble of consulting me about anything anymore and just do what you want."

Sawyer says nothing. What could she say? Neither of them speaks for the rest of the drive home. When they arrive, Paul carries a sleeping Matthew up to bed while Sawyer immediately goes to the kitchen to look out the back window. The lights to the pool house are off, which shouldn't surprise her because Ethan's car wasn't in the driveway when they arrived home. She feels her heart rate speed up. She checks her phone. No calls or texts from Ethan.

Utterly exhausted, Sawyer heads upstairs and gets ready for bed. She's already under the covers scrolling through her phone when Paul comes into their bedroom.

"Matthew woke up as soon as I put him in bed, so I got him changed and lied down with him a bit. He fell back asleep quickly, though," Paul says.

"Thank you."

Paul changes into a T-shirt and flannel pajama bottoms and disappears into the master bathroom to brush his teeth. When he comes back out and climbs into bed with Sawyer, his expression has softened.

"Sawyer, I'm sorry. I know you're just trying to do the right thing. It's just ... there's something about this guy I don't trust. I can't quite put my finger on it. But I shouldn't let my own crazy feelings make me so angry."

A flood of guilt washes over Sawyer. She doesn't know what to say. Paul is such a good man; he trusts her so much, and she doesn't deserve that trust.

"I texted my mom while I was in Matthew's room, and she said of course we can invite Ethan. So go ahead and extend the invitation."

Sawyer fights back tears. "He's not even here, Paul. His car is gone and his lights are off. Maybe he decided to stay at a hotel after all."

"Nah, that guy is smooth. He's probably hooking up with some girl," Paul says, chuckling.

Sawyer feels like she's going to puke. "*Really*, Paul?"

He shrugs. "It's a strong possibility! Why don't you just text him and invite him?"

"If he comes back, I will in the morning," Sawyer says. And she turns and switches off her bedside lamp. She just can't deal with this anymore. She also can't deal with the thought of Ethan with another woman, as unfair as she knows that is.

"All right—whatever you say," Paul replies. He rolls over onto his side and goes to sleep.

Chapter 44

"MOMMY, DADDY! LET'S GO WATCH THE PARADE!" Matthew shouts the next morning, bouncing on the bed between Sawyer and Paul. Sawyer opens her eyes and sleepily checks the time on her phone. 7:21 a.m.

"Buddyyyyy," she whines. "The parade doesn't come on until 9! Why don't we all go back to sleep for a bit?"

"Because I'm hungry!" Matthew says. "Can we have pancakes?"

Sawyer sighs and glances at Paul. He's either sleeping through the commotion or pretending to be asleep. "All right, kiddo—let's go make some pancakes," she says.

She pulls on her robe and follows Matthew down the stairs. "Why don't you go watch some TV while Mommy makes coffee and gets breakfast ready?" Sawyer asks.

"OK!" Matthew says happily and bolts into the family room.

Sawyer turns on the kitchen lights and when she looks out the sliding door, she's surprised to see the lights on in the pool house. She heads to the front of the house and opens the front door. Sure enough, Ethan's Civic is parked at the end of the driveway. Sawyer wonders what time he got in.

Her heart pounding, she heads back to the kitchen and picks up her phone.

Good morning, she writes. **Got home at 9:30 last night and your car was gone. Everything OK?**

Then she realizes how desperate the second line sounds and deletes it.

Thanksgiving plans? she types instead.

She's about to put the phone back down on the counter when she sees the three dots appear that indicate Ethan is writing back.

It depends. Are you inviting me somewhere?

Sawyer breaks into a wide smile despite herself.

My in-laws' in Brooklyn. They do Thanksgiving every year. They told me they would love for you to come.

The three dots appear again, then disappear, then return again.

You're kidding me, right? I can't do that.

Sawyer feels her heart drop. How silly was she to think Ethan would be so eager to spend Thanksgiving with her that he'd happily go to her *husband's parents' house?* She desperately tries to think of what to say and then decides it may be best to try to level the playing field.

Well, I guess you could always spend Thanksgiving with whatever woman you were with last night. Saw that you were out late.

It takes a while for the dots to return, and Sawyer starts to panic that she'd gone too far. But eventually he responds.

Which woman? he replies. **There were lots of them at the food bank where I was volunteering to pack Thanksgiving meals.**

Sawyer's eyes widen. She hates herself for assuming Paul was right about Ethan being with a woman. She can't believe Ethan—her son's father—was volunteering at a food bank only two days after losing his home and business in a fire. She's not worthy of him, or of Paul, or of anyone.

I am an ass. I wouldn't want to spend Thanksgiving with me either. I'm sorry, she writes.

She assumes the matter is closed, but then Ethan writes back. **There is no one I'd rather spend Thanksgiving with, even if it will be awkward AF. Just give me the time and address and I'll be there.**

Sawyer exhales with relief. **Nonsense,** she types. **You can ride with us. We're leaving at 1 p.m. But you'll have to listen to Matthew talk about Pokémon the whole way.**

Ethan responds instantly. **Sounds awesome. I'll teach him everything I know.**

Chapter 45

AT 12:57 P.M., SAWYER BUCKLES MATTHEW INTO HIS car seat and climbs into the passenger seat next to Paul. "He should be out here any minute," she says.

"Who?" asks Matthew from the backseat.

Sawyer turns around. "Remember Ethan, from the other day?"

Matthew's eyes light up.

"You mean the Pokémon guy? Yeah! Is he coming to Grandma and Grandpa's with us?"

"He sure is!" Sawyer replies, at which Matthew shouts, "Yay!" and throws his arms up in the air. Sawyer glances at Paul just in time to see a flash of jealousy cross his face.

Just then Ethan appears from the side of the house holding a large stuffed Pikachu in one arm and a shopping bag hanging over the other.

"Jesus Christ," Paul mutters under his breath as he pushes the button to release the child locks. Sawyer's heart races as Ethan opens the car door and slides in behind her.

"Hey there, little man!" he says to Matthew. "Mind if Pikachu sits between us?"

Matthew gasps, takes the Pikachu into his arms, and hugs it. "Is this for *me*?" he asks incredulously.

"It sure is, little man," Ethan replies. Then he leans forward. "I hope it's OK with you guys. I couldn't resist getting it for him when I saw it."

"It's fine," Paul and Sawyer say in unison, though Sawyer says it genuinely while Paul says it through gritted teeth.

"Great!" Ethan says. He leans back and puts his seat belt on. "I also picked up a pie at the grocery store. Sorry—short notice and I'm not much of a baker."

"No, it's fine—Paul's parents will love it!" Sawyer says, glancing at her husband. His eyes are trained on the road.

There's a lot of Thanksgiving traffic, and it takes nearly two hours to arrive at Paul's parents' house. Matthew, who'd normally be complaining the whole way and asking incessantly when they're going to be there, is happy as a clam the entire drive. He and Ethan talk nonstop—about Pokémon, about baseball, about what Matthew wants from Santa for Christmas. As they gab, Sawyer's heart melts more and more, and the vein on the side of Paul's face bulges more and more. Then Ethan and Matthew start to tell jokes, and their guffaw is so similar, Sawyer fears that Paul and Ethan are finally going to figure things out.

"Hey, Matthew—what do you call a pig that does karate?" Ethan asks.

"What?"

"A pork chop!"

Matthew giggles so hard it makes Ethan giggle, which then makes Sawyer giggle, and soon the three of them are doubled over with laughter.

"Hey, Matthew!" Paul cuts in loudly. "Why did the turkey cross the road?"

"Why?"

"Because it was Thanksgiving, and he wanted everyone to think he was a chicken!"

The laughter stops. "Huh? Matthew asks. "I don't get it."

"You know—you eat turkey on Thanksgiving? And he didn't want people to know he was a turkey so they wouldn't eat him ..."

There's more silence until Ethan finally speaks. "Good one, man."

Paul takes a hard swerve to the left to switch lanes. "Why don't we all quiet down now so Matthew can take a nap?"

"But, Daddy! I'm having so much fun with Ethan!"

"Well, you went to bed late last night. You need a nap!"

Sawyer glances into the backseat. Matthew's eyes are getting watery, and Ethan throws his hands up in defeat. "Sorry," Ethan says.

"Paul, come on. Matthew's having a great time, and he hasn't complained once about the drive," Sawyer says, placing her hand on her husband's upper back. She feels Paul's shoulders stiffen.

"Fine, then," he snaps. "You and Ethan can deal with him when he's having a meltdown in the middle of Thanksgiving dinner."

Sawyer opens her mouth to respond, but instead she crosses her arms, leans back in her seat and closes her eyes. They spend the next 30 minutes of the drive in a tense silence. Matthew doesn't nap, but instead gazes out the window dreamily, clutching his beloved Pikachu.

Chapter 46

THANKSGIVING AT SAWYER'S IN-LAWS' HOUSE GOES better than she could have imagined—for everyone except Paul, that is. When they arrive, Matthew can't wait to introduce everyone to Pikachu—and to Ethan. Ethan tries to help in the kitchen but winds up spending most of his pre-mealtime with Matthew and Jasmine, indulging their every whim. He does Mad Libs with them (dutifully saying words like "fart" and "poop" when they ask for verbs and nouns), lets Jasmine teach him hand-clapping games and at one point even pretends to be a pony and crawls around on the floor with them on his back. Paul watches football in the family room with his dad and Melissa's husband, avoiding Ethan altogether, until Matthew pulls out Connect 4. After Ethan lets both children win, Paul joins them and declares that he is the Connect 4 champion. He does not let Matthew win, he does not let Jasmine win and he sure as hell isn't going to let Ethan win—except Ethan handily beats him seven times in a row, until Sawyer appears and says it's time to put the game away and have dinner.

"I want to sit next to Ethan!" Jasmine declares.

"No, *I* want to!" Matthew says. "He's staying at *my* house!"

"Now, now, kids," Melissa says. "I'm sure Ethan would be happy to sit in between both of you."

"Absolutely!" Ethan says. "I love the kids' table!"

During dinner, Ethan is charming, charismatic and friendly. He makes everyone except Paul laugh, he asks questions and listens intently to the answers, and he says many times how delicious all the food is. After dinner, when everyone has finished cleaning up, Paul's dad invites Ethan to watch more football with them in the family room, much to Paul's dismay.

"Oh my *gosh*, Sawyer—that man is amazing!" Melissa says once the men are in the other room. "Do you think he'd like Jackie? He wouldn't mind that she has two kids, right? He's so good with Matthew and Jasmine!"

Sawyer barely keeps from scowling. Jackie is Melissa's gorgeous best friend who got divorced a year ago. No way in hell is she going to let Melissa introduce Ethan to her.

"I don't think he's ready to date anyone right now, Melissa. He's just had his life turned upside down."

"Oh, I don't mean *now*, silly," Melissa says. "But we're definitely going to have to try to hook them up once he's back on his feet."

"Um … yeah. We'll see, I guess."

Melissa gazes into the family room.

"Gosh, he really is adorable," she swoons. "He's got that blond hair and those deep blue eyes, just like Matthew!"

Sawyer freezes with fear. But then Melissa says, "I always thought I'd end up with a blond-haired guy. Instead, I got my Latin lover—just like you. Ha!"

"Um, yeah …" Sawyer replies.

"Gotta love those Latin men!" Melissa says, giggling.

The drive home that evening is quicker, but just as fraught with tension. Ethan and Matthew both fall asleep in the backseat, and Sawyer pretends to sleep as well. She doesn't know why she feels the need to pretend, though. She suspects that even if she were wide awake, Paul would have nothing to say to her.

Chapter 47

THE NEXT MONTH IS A WHIRLWIND AS THE CHAOS of the Christmas season settles in. Sawyer aces both of her finals and winds up with an A in both classes. Paul spends more hours than usual in the office to prepare for the holiday leave he'll take from December 22 until after the New Year. Sawyer suspects he's avoiding Ethan as well.

Sawyer and Matthew find themselves spending a lot of time with Ethan. During the week after Thanksgiving, Ethan volunteers to watch Matthew after school on Tuesday, Thursday and Friday while Sawyer is holed up in her office studying and working on her final projects. He also watches him on Wednesday when she has to leave for her last class, and Paul calls to say he is stuck in traffic. Once school ends for Sawyer, she and Ethan go Christmas shopping and run holiday errands, and he even hangs Christmas lights on the house because Paul is too busy at work to do it.

One day, Sawyer brings Ethan out to brunch with her and Ava, much to Ava's chagrin. Sawyer believes that if Ava meets Ethan, she'll realize what a wonderful guy he is and be more understanding of Sawyer's predicament. But Ava, fiercely loyal to Paul, is incredibly rude to Ethan, which in turn makes Ethan obsess over what he did to offend her.

By the time Christmas Eve rolls around, Sawyer is feeling more distant from Paul than ever. When Paul heads to the store to buy wine to bring to Sawyer's parents' house for Christmas Eve dinner, she tells Matthew she'll be right in and heads out to the pool house. She knocks on the door, and when Ethan answers, she lets herself in.

"Sawyer!" he says. "Everything OK?"

Sawyer begins pacing back and forth. "I don't know, Ethan. Paul is starting to get really upset about … everything. I think he's starting to suspect that something is going on between us."

Ethan sits down on the couch. "But nothing is going on between us, Sawyer. You made that very clear that afternoon in my apartment." (His voice cracks when he says the word "apartment.")

"But something *did* happen!" Sawyer says.

Ethan sighs. "Sawyer, it was just a kiss …"

"We said we loved each other."

"We were being honest."

"Ethan, come on. I feel like I'm the least honest person on this planet," Sawyer says.

Ethan stands up again. "Sawyer, I'm sorry I put you in the position to feel that way. I really am. Like I said, I wanted to be honest with you about how I felt about you—how I *still* feel about you. But I respected your choice, and I've been nothing but respectful of your marriage. And I don't want to cause any other problems between you and Paul. So after the holidays, I'll leave. I'll move to a hotel. It'll only be a couple more months until the apartment and studio are ready, anyway."

Sawyer starts to pace again. "No, Ethan … stop. You don't have to leave."

"So then what were you coming here to tell me, Sawyer? You tell me I'm causing problems between you and Paul, but you don't want me to leave. What would you like me to do, then?"

She can't look at him. She starts to cry. "I want you to not come to my parents' house this evening," she says. "And I want you to not come to my house for Christmas tomorrow. I'm sorry, Ethan."

His eyes widen. He looks stricken. "Are you serious?" he asks. "Is that really what you want?"

She cries harder. "Yes, it is! I mean, no. No, of course it's not what I want. But I think it's what needs to happen."

He sits on the couch again and stares at the floor. Then he looks back up at her, his jaw set. "I won't come for Christmas tomorrow, OK? But I *am* coming tonight. Please don't stop me."

"Excuse me?" Sawyer asks.

"I told Matthew I would give him the presents I bought him tonight, remember? And that he and I could play with them at your parents' house. He is so excited. Please don't make me disappoint him."

Sawyer freezes, then moves to sit next to Ethan on the couch. He looks at her, and she sees tears in his eyes. "Oh, my God …" she says. "You love him! You really love him, Ethan—don't you?"

He nods and begins to cry. "I do, Sawyer. God, that kid is so amazing. I'll leave tomorrow. I will. But please don't kick me out of Matthew's life completely. Please."

Now Sawyer is sobbing, and she doesn't know what to do. Should she tell Ethan everything—that he is Matthew's biological father? He just said he loves Matthew. She can *see* how much he loves Matthew, and how much Matthew loves him. And maybe … maybe if Paul knows the truth, he'll understand why Sawyer wanted to help Ethan so much.

But no, she's being crazy. Paul would be devastated. Ethan would be so angry. So instead she says, "OK, Ethan. Come with us tonight."

He shakes his head. "I've got presents for everyone, and they won't all fit. I'll just drive my own car there, OK?"

"OK," Sawyer says. She tries to reach over and hug Ethan, but he stiffens.

"Please don't," Ethan says. "Just go, OK? I'll see you later."

"Ok," Sawyer replies. And she leaves the pool house and closes the door gently behind her.

Chapter 48

"DIDN'T YOU TELL HIM WE WERE GETTING HERE AT 3?" Paul asks later that afternoon as he sits with Sawyer in her parents' family room. "It's almost 4."

"Yeah, but dinner isn't until 5," Sawyer replies. "And besides, my parents are really enjoying having Matthew all to themselves."

"Yeah, well, it's pretty rude to show up just in time for dinner, isn't it?"

Sawyer is about to defend Ethan when the doorbell rings. She practically catapults herself off her parents' couch. "That's him now!" she says.

Matthew jumps up from the kitchen table, where he's in the middle of a game of Candy Land with his grandparents. "I think it's Ethan!" he shouts. "Can I answer the door, Grandma?"

"You may certainly come with me," Sawyer's mom replies.

Sawyer hangs back and watches while her mother and Matthew open the door. She expects to see Ethan standing on the doorstep. Instead, she sees a paunchy Santa Claus holding a sack of presents over his shoulder.

"Ho, ho, ho! *Merry Christmas*!" Santa Claus bellows. "I came a little early this year to bring you some extra presents because you've been so good!"

"SANTA!" Matthew shouts, and starts jumping up and down and clapping his hands.

Sawyer's mother looks confused, but she tentatively lets Santa Claus in, much to Matthew's delight. Sawyer quickly steps forward and sees those familiar blue eyes staring at her from above the fake beard. She gasps in surprise before a bolt of panic shoots through her.

"Um, Santa!" she says. "Maybe we should go outside! I'm sure you're in a hurry."

Sawyer's father appears from the kitchen. "What's going on?" he asks when he sees Santa. Then he looks toward the family room, where Paul is sitting, with a confused expression on his face.

Every year since Matthew was 2, Paul has dressed up in a Santa Claus costume on Christmas Eve that he keeps at Sawyer's parents' house. That first year, he shared that his own father had done it for him and Melissa every year when they were kids, and that it was a tradition he always wanted to pass on. And now here is Ethan in a Santa suit. Sawyer starts to shuffle everyone towards the front door when Paul steps into the foyer and spots Santa Claus. His look of surprise quickly changes to contempt when he realizes who it is in the Santa suit.

"How *dare* you!" he shouts, puffing his chest out and stepping so close to Ethan, he bumps into the stuffing in his belly.

Sawyer tries to step in between them as Matthew bursts into tears. Ethan places the sack of presents on the floor. "Ho, ho, ho, don't worry! I didn't bring you any coal!" he tells Paul, trying his best to sound jovial.

"You had *no right*!" Paul bellows. Then he pulls his arm back and punches Ethan square in the face. Ethan falls backward onto the console table next to the front door, knocking over three picture frames that shatter into pieces as they hit the floor. Sawyer screams, and Matthew starts to pound on Paul's back.

"Daddy! Stop beating up Santa!" he yells.

Ethan wobbles to his feet and takes a blow at Paul, who ducks out of the way and yanks Santa's beard off. The scene explodes into chaos as the two men fight, stuffing spilling out of the bottom of the Santa suit and on to the floor. It takes Sawyer and both of her parents to finally pull Paul off Ethan, while Matthew covers his ears in the corner and screams.

"*Stop it—both of you*!" Sawyer screams. "It's *Christmas Eve*, for God's sake!"

Sawyer's mother rushes over to Matthew and scoops him into her arms. "It's OK, sweetheart. You can see now that it's not the real Santa Claus. Don't worry."

"But that's Ethan!" Matthew shouts.

Everyone looks over at Ethan, who's standing against the wall between the console table and the front door with his Santa beard hanging off one side of his face and his suit all disheveled. His nose is bleeding onto the white suite collar. Sawyer lets go of Paul, leaving him with her dad, and rushes to the kitchen to grab some napkins. She brings them back to Ethan.

"For your nose," she says.

He takes them without saying a word and holds them up to his nose. Then Sawyer looks over at Paul, whose eye is already beginning to swell. She once again goes to the kitchen, wraps some ice in a dish towel and brings it Paul. He wordlessly lifts the ice to his eye.

"This stops *now*," Sawyer says sternly. "Paul, my father is going to let go of you, and you are going to stay calm." She nods at her dad, who releases Paul. Paul straightens up and begins to adjust his sweater with his free hand.

"Mom, Dad … would you mind taking Matthew to the basement for a bit while I have a chat with Paul and Ethan?" she asks.

Sawyer's parents exchange a concerned look.

"It's OK, Mr. and Mrs. Reynolds," Ethan says. "I know this evening hasn't gotten off to a good start, but I promise you don't have to worry about anything else. And I'll clean all of this up."

"All right … but don't be too long. The roast only has another 30 minutes or so to cook, and I've got to warm up the side dishes," Sawyer's mom says.

"Don't worry—this won't take long," Sawyer replies.

"Come on, sweetheart," Mrs. Reynolds says to Matthew. "Grandpa and I will let you open one of your presents before dinner!"

Chapter 49

WHEN THE THREE OF THEM HEAD DOWN TO THE basement, Sawyer leads Paul and Ethan to the sitting room. Ethan now has one of the tissues shoved up his nose and has removed the Santa hat, beard, jacket and boots. He is now in a white Hanes T-shirt, the Santa pants and candy cane-striped socks. He sits in one of two armchairs facing the settee. Paul settles onto the settee across from Ethan, still holding the dish towel of ice to his right eye and glaring at Ethan with his left eye. Sawyer slides the other chair between them so that she is sitting perpendicular to them. She takes a deep breath and steels herself. *This is it*, she thinks. *It's time to tell the truth about everything.*

"Paul, can I explain to Ethan why you got so upset?" she asks.

"Where would you even begin?" Paul sneers.

Sawyer sighs and turns to Ethan. "Ethan, it's Paul's tradition every Christmas Eve to dress like Santa and bring Matthew his first present. He usually does it after dinner while we are getting ready to exchange gifts with my parents. It's something his dad used to do for him and his sister."

Ethan looks genuinely remorseful. "Oh, my God—I'm so sorry, Paul. I totally overstepped, and I didn't mean to."

"Man, don't give me that!" Paul says, removing the dish towel from his eye and placing it down next to him, where the wetness begins to seep into the settee. "You've been overstepping since the day you started staying in the pool house!"

To Sawyer's relief, Ethan remains calm. "How, Paul? How have I been overstepping? I've been nothing but grateful to you for your hospitality."

"Oh, please!" Paul sputters. "The damn Pikachu. The Christmas lights. All the time you've been spending with my wife!"

Ethan turns to look at Sawyer, waiting for her to say something. She looks back at him and gives him a slight nod. Then she takes another deep breath. "Paul, you didn't trust Ethan from the beginning. You made that very clear. And you were right not to trust him. He hasn't been completely honest with you. But it was because I didn't want him to be."

Paul's face screws up again in anger and panic. "What the hell are you talking about?" he asks, looking from Sawyer to Ethan and back again.

Sawyer turns to Ethan. "And I haven't been honest with you either, Ethan. I haven't been honest with either of you."

Ethan looks genuinely surprised, but says nothing. Sawyer turns back to Paul.

"Paul, I lied to you when I said I didn't know Ethan before I took his class. I did know Ethan. I … hooked up with him a long time ago. It was just one night."

Paul's jaw clenches, and he turns to look out the window. Sawyer swallows. "Paul," she says, struggling to maintain her composure. "Paul … please look at me."

He finally looks back at her. She can see his jaw trembling. She wants so badly to sit next to him—to take him into her arms and tell him everything will be OK. But she has no idea if it will be. All she knows is that it's time for him to know the truth. She looks at him meaningfully and says, "It was six and a half years ago when we hooked up, Paul …"

He stares back at her, and she sees the moment that it hits him. The moment he understands what she's trying to tell him.

Sawyer can't bear it. She looks back at Ethan. He looks sad and apologetic, but she can see that he hasn't yet figured out what Paul already has. "Ethan …" she says. "It was six and a half years ago …"

Ethan stares back at her blankly, and Paul looks at her. "You mean *he* doesn't know, either?"

She shakes her head, and that appears to soften the blow just a tiny bit for Paul.

"Don't know what, Sawyer?" Ethan asks.

Paul looks back at him. "Don't you get it, man? You hooked up with her six and a half years ago. Matthew turns six in a few months. He's got blond hair, blue eyes …"

Ethan's eyes grow as large as saucers, and he slowly brings his hands to his mouth. Tears immediately spring to his eyes and run down the sides of his face.

"I'm so sorry …" Sawyer says. "You had a right to know he was your biological son. I should have told you as soon as class started …"

But Ethan's face breaks into the widest smile Sawyer has ever seen— like a kid who's entered Disney World for the first time and is gazing up at Cinderella's castle. He is openly weeping now and not the slightest bit self-conscious about it.

"Oh, my God, Sawyer. Oh, my God! How could I not have seen it? The kid is my little clone. Oh, my God! I have a son!"

Sawyer turns back to Paul. He is also weeping, but his are tears of agony. He looks at her with such sad eyes, she can't even stand it. Sawyer begins to cry too.

"Paul, *you* are Matthew's father," she says. "Do you hear me? *You* are his father."

She looks at Ethan. "Do you understand that?"

"Oh, *man*!" Ethan says. "Yes, of course I do. Absolutely. I just want to be a part of Matthew's life. I have no intention of trying to steal him away. Paul, you're his dad, man."

Paul is distraught, shaking with the torture of this newfound knowledge. Sawyer gets up and rushes next to him, holding him as he rocks back and forth.

"Paul, honey, you heard him," she says. "We can figure out how to make this work."

"I should have seen it," Paul splutters. "These past couple of months, I've felt like the damn third wheel around you two and Matthew. He loves Ethan! I could never compare …"

"Paul, that's not true," Ethan says calmly. "I see the way that boy looks at you. I hear the way he talks about you. That boy worships you, Paul. You're the only father he's ever known. Me … I'm just the fun uncle."

They all sit in silence for a few excruciating minutes, Sawyer rubbing Paul's back as he takes big, snotty gulps of air. When he finally calms down, she looks across at Ethan, who once again has his face in his hands. She knows she should remain there next to her husband and continue to support him, to show him that they're a united front. But her heart aches for Ethan, too, and she feels an overwhelming pull toward him. She crosses the room, perches on the arm of his chair and begins to rub his back as well. She looks down at him, trying to ascertain what he is thinking, but he won't even look at her.

"Holy, shit," she hears from across the room.

She looks up to see Paul staring at her and Ethan with recognition in his eyes. She begins to panic. "Paul …" she says.

He holds up a hand. "Don't, Sawyer. Just tell me—how long has it been going on?"

Now Ethan looks up at her. She struggles to think of what to say to buy time. "What are you talking about, Paul?" she asks.

"How long have you two been having an affair?" he sneers.

Sawyer begins to shake her head vigorously. "No. Paul, no. Ethan and I are not having an affair."

Paul picks up the now soggy dish towel from the crook of the settee's arm and flings it across the room, where it hits the wall and slides to the floor, leaving a streak of water behind. "Don't lie to me anymore, Sawyer!" he says. "You've told enough lies! Don't you think I deserve the truth?"

Sawyer looks again at Ethan, whose face remains stoic. She sighs and turns back to Paul.

"We're not having an affair, Paul," she repeats. "We kissed. Once. The day of the yoga workshop."

Paul presses his temples with his fingers, and she sees his Adam's apple bob as he takes a hard swallow. "The day we watched *The Polar Express* with *our son*," he says through gritted teeth. "You kissed this guy and then came home and watched *The Polar Express* with me and our son, like nothing happened."

Sawyer feels the anxiety begin to consume her, but she wills herself to stay calm. She wipes away tears and shakes her head. "No, Paul … it wasn't like nothing happened. I've had to live with it every day."

"Then why didn't you tell me?"

More tears, more wiping of her cheeks. "Because I had to finish Ethan's class," she says. "Because he's Matthew's biological dad. And I knew if I told you, you'd never let us see him again."

Paul stares into Sawyer's eyes, boring into her soul. It is at that moment that Sawyer realizes the husband she believed didn't understand her at all, actually knows her quite well. So well, in fact, that he can see in that moment that Sawyer loves Ethan. She can't hide it. And if he asks her, she will have to tell him the truth.

But he doesn't ask her. He doesn't have to. He just takes a deep breath and stands up as the oven timer begins to chime from the kitchen. Sawyer stands up too. Ethan remains seated in his Santa Claus pants.

"Paul …" Sawyer says. "I can turn off the oven and tell my parents we all need to talk more …"

But Paul begins to walk toward the kitchen in a determined manner. Then he stops and turns back to Sawyer and Ethan resolutely. "Sawyer, show him where the bathroom is so he can clean himself up," he says. "I'll go help your parents, and we're going to have a nice Christmas Eve dinner. For our son."

"Paul …" Ethan says, standing up.

"We're not going to talk about this anymore," Paul says. "We're going to give Matthew a good Christmas Eve. Go get cleaned up."

Chapter 50

Three Months Later

SAWYER SHIVERS AS SHE LEAVES GRETA'S AND GETS into her car. She had class tonight and then went for a quick bite with Myra, the girl who'd been in Ethan's class with her the prior semester. She and Myra had been paired up for a project and decided to grab a bite at Greta's while starting to plan.

Sawyer immediately turns on her heated seat. She usually doesn't mind March because it means spring is right around the corner, but this March has been particularly brutal with record cold temperatures, and Sawyer is over it. April is a week away, and it still feels like February. She's glad they decided to hold Matthew's 6th birthday party, which is in two weeks, at an indoor trampoline park.

Sawyer merges onto the highway and finds herself lost in thought as she drives. It's been a tough few months as she, Paul and Ethan have adjusted to their new reality. Once Paul and Ethan had time to process everything, the three of them had a big talk one evening after Matthew went to bed about how they'd handle things moving forward. They made the incredibly difficult decision that it was time to be honest with Matthew that Paul wasn't his biological father and that Ethan was. Ethan insisted that Sawyer and Paul tell him alone, that his being there would only make it more confusing for Matthew.

Paul had taken a half day from work the next day so he could pick up Matthew from the bus with Sawyer. They took him home, gave him a Costco chocolate chip cookie—his favorite—for a snack and delivered the news. They were so prepared for him to freak out that Sawyer had even started researching child psychologists that morning. But when they finished, he simply looked up at them and asked if he could have another cookie. Sawyer and Paul laughed out loud with a mixture of relief and amazement that their 5-year-old son was smart enough to use news like this to wrangle an extra cookie out of his parents. Once they obliged and gave him the second cookie, Paul asked if he had any questions.

"Well, since you're Daddy, what should I call Ethan?" Matthew asked.

Paul looked at Sawyer, who shrugged her shoulders. "Well … you can keep calling him Ethan, if you want," Paul said. "Or you can call him Uncle Ethan."

"OK," Matthew replied nonchalantly. "And is Uncle Ethan still going to live in the pool house?"

That question pains Sawyer to this day. With the renovations on Ethan's studio and apartment so close to being finished—and Ethan set to move back home at the end of April—she dreaded telling Matthew that Ethan would be moving away.

"For a few more months," Paul told him. "But when the construction people finish fixing his apartment, he's going to move back home."

"But the pool house *is* his home!" Matthew insisted. "Why can't he just keep living there?"

"Well, honey, he lives on top of where he works," Sawyer said.

"He can drive to work, like Daddy does!" Matthew said.

At that point, Paul and Sawyer decided to change the subject, and thankfully, Matthew had moved on. But now that Ethan is set to move in only a few weeks, Sawyer is a ball of anxiety again. The truth is, she is going to miss Ethan too. The last few months were hard, but they are all in a good place now. Because of the marriage counseling she and Paul started right after the new year, they have a newfound understanding of each other and are communicating so much better. He has come to accept the fact that she loves Ethan, too, but miraculously, he trusts her not to cross the line again. It's an arrangement that no one in their lives can understand—not her parents, not Paul's family, not Ava nor Mike. But they've all acknowledged what a great guy Ethan is and that he is Matthew's biological father.

"If it works for all of you, who are we to question it?" Sawyer's mom had told her. "Your father and I support you no matter what."

"You don't know how lucky you are that Paul has been so understanding about all of this," Ava had said. "You better not screw things up again."

Paul's parents and sister had been a bit harder to convince, and they still haven't completely come around. But Sawyer is Matthew's mother, and they know she isn't going anywhere, so they promised to do their best to be accepting of everything.

As for Paul and Ethan, they're not going to be best friends, but they coexist. Ethan spends time with Matthew every day after school and retreats back to the pool house before Paul gets home from work. Sawyer usually keeps herself busy doing other things while Ethan and

Matthew are together, even though she wants so badly to be with the two of them. It's out of respect for Paul and the extraordinary amount of grace he is giving them.

Sawyer knows how much easier things will be for Paul once Ethan moves out. She can't imagine what it must feel like for him to know that this man she loves, who is the biological father of his son, is always right there in his backyard. She knows—and she's admitted to Paul many times—that *she* wouldn't be able to do it if the situation were reversed. But at the same time, it will be heartbreaking for Matthew not to see Ethan every day, and for Sawyer to know he's so far away. Just knowing he is right there has brought her an indescribable level of comfort. And will it be harder or easier for Ethan? She doesn't know. She imagines it must be very painful to be around her and not be able to hold her or kiss her. But she also knows how much he will miss Matthew.

Sawyer pulls into the driveway a short time later and feels the familiar shot of warmth upon seeing Paul's BMW and Ethan's Civic side by side in the driveway.

My two men, she thinks to herself. *My two loves.*

She walks up to the porch with her tote bag on her arm. She expects to do her usual routine when she gets inside—wave at the pool house through the kitchen window (even though Ethan never sees her), then go upstairs to Paul and Matthew. But when she steps in through the front door, she hears laughter coming from the family room. She raises her eyebrows and quickly kicks off her shoes and hangs her coat in the closet. Then she hurries into the family room.

Sawyer's mouth drops at what she sees—Ethan and Paul sitting on opposite corners of the sectional with beers in their hand. Four more empty beer bottles sit on top of the large, round coffee table. The

Yankees game is on TV, but the volume is turned all the way down. Both men look up at her when she enters the room.

"Sawyer!" Paul says. "Where have you been, young lady?"

"Yes, young lady—class ended a long time ago!" Ethan says.

The two of them burst into buzzed laughter, but Sawyer is confused. She looks back and forth between the two men with her mouth hanging open. That makes them laugh even harder. They're clearly enjoying this moment.

"Look at her face!" Paul says.

"Like a deer in headlights!" Ethan pants.

"Very funny," Sawyer says, crossing her arms. "Will one of you explain to me what is going on here?"

This makes Ethan snort, which causes beer to shoot out of his nose, which makes Paul completely lose his mind. The two men are now doubled over with laughter, struggling to breathe.

"What the *heck*?" Sawyer asks, which only makes things even worse.

She turns and is about to leave the room when Paul takes a few deep breaths and calls her back. "OK, OK, we'll stop," he says. "Come sit—we need to talk to you."

She looks back at Ethan, who is taking a few heaving breaths in his attempt to stop laughing. Then she walks over and sits right in the middle of the sectional, equally distant from both men.

"OK, you got it out of your system. Now tell me what the heck is going on."

She looks back and forth between them, silently daring them to start laughing again, but they both know better. Paul leans forward and places his empty beer bottle on the coffee table. Ethan gets up and does the same, then sits back down in his corner. Sawyer doesn't know whether to feel frightened about what's to come or ecstatic that they're enjoying each other's company.

"So, Ethan and I have had a nice long chat tonight," Paul says.

"You did?" Sawyer asks.

"We did. He came in and had pizza with me and Matthew, since you had an earlier class this evening."

Sawyer opens her mouth to speak, but no words come out. She doesn't know how to react to this news. She's both nervous and delighted about Matthew sharing a meal with Ethan and Paul. She also feels a bit jealous that she wasn't there and apprehensive about how Matthew handled the whole thing. As if reading her mind, Ethan speaks up.

"Don't worry—Matthew didn't seem weirded out by it at all," he says. "In fact, I think it was good for him to see Paul and I acting normal and getting along."

Sawyer nods slowly, trying to process everything.

"After I put Matthew to bed, Ethan and I opened some beers and started talking," Paul says. "And what we realized is that we can't change this situation. We can't change the fact that Ethan is Matthew's biological father and that I am his adoptive father. We can't change the fact that we are both madly in love with you and with Matthew, and that Matthew loves us both, and that you love us both."

"You know what they say—if you can't beat 'em, join 'em!" Ethan says with a nervous chuckle.

But Sawyer doesn't laugh. She's too busy trying to figure out what exactly is going on. "What are you two trying to say?" she asks.

Paul puffs out his cheeks and lets out a long exhale. "Look, I'm not going to lie and say I'm happy that you love someone else, and that someone else loves you," Paul says. "I'm not happy about it *at all*. But it is what it is. You can't help the way you feel any more than Ethan can."

Sawyer can't believe what she's hearing. Is she dreaming? She actually pinches her own forearm and winces.

"And I'm not happy that you lied to me about your history with Ethan. I'm not happy that you kept the fact that he's Matthew's biological father from me. And I'm *especially* not happy that the two of you kissed."

Paul's voice cracks on that last line, and Sawyer's heart aches for him.

"But I forgive you," Paul says. "As we've talked about in therapy, forgiveness is a choice. And my choice is to forgive you."

"Why?" Sawyer asks through tears. "Why on Earth would you ever forgive me?"

Now Paul starts crying, and Ethan looks away. "Because I love you, Sawyer," Paul says. "I love our family. I love the life we've built together. And I love Matthew. And I would never want to break up his family or take Ethan away from him. I know I wasn't always the perfect husband, Sawyer. What you did ... the kiss ... it wasn't my fault. That was completely on you. But I also know that marriage takes two, and that someone doesn't just become unhappy on their own."

Sawyer begins to shake her head furiously. "No, Paul—stop it. You are *not* responsible for my actions."

"I know that, Sawyer. But I *am* responsible for not always giving you the attention and affection you deserved. I got complacent."

"It doesn't matter, Paul," Sawyer says. "You were a great husband. You *are* a great husband. It's just ... Ethan and I have a connection I can't explain. And he's Matthew's ..."

"Stop," Paul says, as if it would pain him to hear her finish the sentence. "I know, Sawyer. I understand. This is a unique situation. But I want to make it work. For all of us. And I want to continue being your husband. But I need to know that that's what you want."

I want you both, Sawyer thinks to herself. But she nods her head and says, "Yes, it's what I want." She glances at Ethan, who is staring at the floor. This can't be easy for him to hear.

"OK, then," Paul says. "So that means I can trust that what happened between you and Ethan … the kiss … it's not going to happen again, right? Can you promise me that? Because this is going to be really hard, Sawyer, but it would be downright impossible if I felt like I always had to be looking over my shoulder."

"Yes," Sawyer says. "Yes, I can promise you that."

"Yeah, man," Ethan says. "I love her, but I would never do anything to jeopardize this arrangement. For all of our sakes, and especially for Matthew's sake."

"*What* arrangement?" Sawyer asks, her voice rising an octave.

"Well," Paul says. "I invited Ethan to stay in the pool house even after his renovations are done."

"*What?!*" Sawyer asks.

"I'm going to sell the apartment," Ethan says, "and pay the two of you rent."

"You're kidding me," Sawyer says.

"I'm not," Ethan replies.

"*WHAT?* What about the studio?"

Ethan shrugs. "I'll hire a studio manager, go teach a few classes a week. Maybe eventually I'll sell it and try to open a studio closer to here and get my own place."

"But for now," Paul says, "we both thought it would be best for Matthew if Ethan stays close by. That way we won't have to figure out visitation and everything. And we've proven these past couple of months that with the proper boundaries, this can work."

Sawyer is completely gobsmacked by what she's hearing. Is this for real? Is she really going to be able to continue living with *both* of the men she loves—her husband and her son's biological father?

"Is that a yes?" Paul asks.

Sawyer looks back and forth at the two men and breaks into a wide smile. "Oh my God, yes!" she says. "A thousand times yes!"

Chapter 51

TWO WEEKS LATER, SAWYER WATCHES AS MATTHEW, Paul and Ethan jump like goofballs on a massive trampoline at the trampoline park. Matthew is wearing a shirt that says, "I'm the Birthday Boy!" Paul's shirt says, "I'm the Dad!" And Ethan's shirt says—what else? "Fun Uncle."

Ava steps up beside her. "Mike took Nate over to the baby area, so I finally have a minute to breathe."

When Sawyer doesn't respond, she follows Sawyer's gaze and clicks her tongue. "Unbelievable," she says, shaking her head. "There was a time you thought you'd never be able to find one man. Now you have *two*."

"Oh, please!" Sawyer says. "You make me sound like a polygamist."

"You mean to tell me you wouldn't marry both of them if it were legal?"

"Ava…"

"OK, but you'd totally bang both of them if Paul were on board with it."

"Stop it!" Sawyer says, nudging her friend.

Suddenly, Sawyer hears a loud voice behind them. "OK, ladies. One of you better tell me right away who that mighty fine blond man over there is!"

Sawyer whirls around. "Oh my gosh—you came!" she says.

"Aunt Grace!" Ava says, throwing her arms around the older woman. Aunt Grace is wearing a tight leopard-print shirt tucked into studded jeans and gold spike heels. Her hair is now dyed jet black, and she's got on her full face of makeup, including red lipstick.

"Of course I came!" Aunt Grace says. "You ladies know I would never miss a party!"

Sawyer chuckles. "I think you have a different kind of party in mind."

"Now, any party with a man as fine as *that* man is my kind of party. Is one of you gonna tell me who he is or what?"

"Oh, that's just Sawyer's baby daddy," Ava says nonchalantly.

"Say what, now?" Aunt Grace says.

Sawyer decides to play along. "Yep. That's Matthew's biological father. And you may have actually met him! He was a bartender at Ava and Mike's wedding."

"Well, I was a bit preoccupied with my own hunk of meat that night," Aunt Grace says, cackling.

Sawyer's mom appears. "Grace! When did you get here?"

"Just a few minutes ago. Fashionably late, as always."

"Well, it's good to see you. Sawyer, the party planner told me it's time to sing happy birthday and have cupcakes. Why don't you start gathering all the parents and kids and sending them to the party room?"

"OK," Sawyer says. "Ava, you go grab Mike and Nate, and I'll start gathering the other guests."

"And I'll go get your husband and that dreamboat next to him," Aunt Grace says.

Ten minutes later, Sawyer, Paul and Matthew are standing behind the Pikachu cake that Ethan had ordered, surrounded by Matthew's friends and their family. When the birthday song is over and Matthew blows out the candles, the three of them pose for pictures. Sawyer is about to lean down to remove the candle from the cake when her mom says, "Wait! Ethan, why don't you get in a picture?"

Ethan looks stunned. "Are you sure?"

Sawyer looks up at Paul, who nods his head. "Yeah, man," he says. "Come on and get in one."

Ethan walks around the table and stands on the other side of Sawyer, with a beaming Matthew in front of them. Mrs. Reynolds snaps a photo of this crazy, unconventional family of four. It's a photo Sawyer treasures for the rest of her life.

ABOUT THE AUTHOR

 Candace Parker is the author of the children's books *My Vote Counts* and *Hazel's Holiday* as well as the romance novel *Give Me Ten Days: Every Breakup Doesn't Have to Break You*. Candace enjoys traveling to places with beautiful beaches and binge-watching shows that leave her begging for more at the finale.

Lightning Source UK Ltd.
Milton Keynes UK
UKHW020646180722
406010UK00010B/1192